Alpha's Magical Mate

By
Gretchen S.B.

For information contact :
GretchenS.B.author@gmail.com
http://www.GretchenSB.com

Previously published on Kindle Vella

Acknowledgments

Thank you to my editor Lacie at Pelican Proofing. You made this book readable for everyone.

Thank you to Get Covers for giving this book such a beautiful cover.

As always, thank you to my friends and family who cheer me on as I work toward my dream of being a full-time author.

Last of all, but not least, is the Hubster. Although he hates to be mentioned, he deserves credit for all his support.

Chapter 1

Three years earlier

Charlotte

Finally, after the week she'd had, a little luck came her way. The full moon above her sang to her wolf, coaxing it out of her as Charlotte prepared for her first shift. Though early June, it was no hotter than seventy degrees outside. Meaning she wouldn't have to worry about cutting her first wolf run short due to the heat.

Charlotte could feel her family behind her. The excitement she felt from them was comforting for both her and her budding wolf. While in the back of her mind she still worried Brian, the alpha's son, would appear and cause problems for her, it didn't overshadow the joy she felt.

She could smell the surrounding trees. This wasn't her native forest, but the smell and sense of nature was a cooling balm to the frustration of having to relocate last-minute. Charlotte took one deep breath before removing her dress and felt her body change. Relief flowed through her. She would not be just a witch with a wolf trapped inside her, a problem that could happen with hybrids, but both a wolf and a witch.

Charlotte was a hybrid. Witch powers popped up on her mother's side and flourished in Charlotte. Witch abilities were not dominate like werewolf genes, so the two don't manifest together often. Werewolves tended to look down on those with hybrid blood. For some, it was proof that a particular line of wolves was not strong enough to overtake the witch genetics. Others thought of it as impure.

Due to these prejudices popping up in their own pack, Charlotte's parents chose to keep her magic a secret. Only their extended family knew about Charlotte's true nature, but that did not mean Charlotte and her parents were not always on edge, especially when, as a teen, she had several slip-ups. Her little secret was why she shifted in unfamiliar woods and not their home territory for her first shift.

The week before

It started with her early morning shift at the bakery in Crescent Falls, a small human-run city, just north of North Bend, Washington, technically in pack territory, though the humans were unaware werewolves existed.

Starting before 3:30 a.m. meant Charlotte beat her coworkers in by two hours. She took advantage of this by blasting her music, sipping from her large coffee, and kneading a sweet bread dough. When she glanced out one of the large back windows—it was still dark out—she got an eerie sense of being watched from the small wooded area across the back alley. As she watched, a figure stepped out of the tree line across the alley, just on the edge of the asphalt. Charlotte's heart rate picked up as she coiled her fingers around the rolling pin on the counter next to her. As far as weapons went, it wasn't much, but it was better than nothing.

Her first shift wouldn't be for another week; while she might be stronger than the average human, she would be nothing compared to a fully grown werewolf. She might be able to get one defensive spell off before he attacked. Taking a shaky breath, she began pooling power in her left hand. The energy sparked and vibrated, eager to be used.

The back door to the shop was locked, but that would mean nothing to a werewolf. Raising all the bravado she could, Charlotte stepped to the window and glared at the interloper. She was careful to keep her hands below the window as they shook from nerves and magic.

Something deep within her told her this was not simply a werewolf out for a morning run or getting up from a drunken night in the woods. Alpha Alexander had drilled into them from the time they were pups that no one was to shift this close to the human city.

As she glowered out the window, he took a step forward, entering the area within the security lights. Brian; that caught her off-guard. What was the alpha of the Crescent Falls pack's son doing here at this time of morning? He continued to stand several beats, watching her. His expression was dark and menacing, clearly threatening her.

Unnerved and angry, he was trying to intimidate her. Charlotte finally wrenched herself from the window, took the four quick strides to the back door, and yanked it open. She didn't know what he was doing there, at three-thirty in the morning. He was of higher rank than her, but not alpha yet;

even if he was, that'd give him no right to threaten her.

Charlotte leaned out the door to see farther in either direction, scanning both the wooded area and the alley, but Brian was gone. If her gut hadn't been so sure it was Brian, she would've thought she hallucinated the whole thing. Growling, Charlotte pushed it aside and got back to work.

— — — — — — — —

The incident slipped her mind until the next afternoon, when she and her cousin Cassie were in another part of downtown, shopping for Charlotte's birthday dress. Since the twenty-fifth birthday was a big deal, a wolf's family threw a big party, inviting family and friends. Charlotte's party would be fifty family members, most from the Crescent Falls pack, but those from other packs were making the trek out as well.

Charlotte appraised an emerald green dress in the mirror that showcased her long, curly, auburn hair beautifully when she realized she was being watched. Tilting her head, she saw Brain out the front window of the store, yet again, watching her from across the street. While some female wolves her age might've been flattered by the attention, it set off alarm bells for Charlotte. Without looking away from Brian, she elbowed Cassie in the side.

"Ooof, what, Char?" Cassie huffed.

Charlotte jutted her chin across the street to where Brian stood. "That's the second time in as many days I've seen Brian standing outside of a store, watching me."

Cassie shifted her gaze, saw Brian, and returned her attention to Charlotte. "Okay." She elongated the 'a'. "Does this come off as attractive or creepy?"

Werewolves had some interesting courting rituals compared to human society. One prospective lover or mate stalking the other was a sign of prowess—that they were such an excellent hunter they could find you anywhere.

That, however, was not Charlotte's cup of tea. "Creepy, we find it creepy. He was standing in the alley outside the bakery at 3:30 a.m. yesterday. It's not like he was there coincidentally."

Cassie leaned her head back, frowning. "Okay, yeah, that's weird. Will you confront him about it? I mean, best-case scenario, he's trying to court you and sucking at it. He could see this as attractive behavior," she warned, waving her arm in his general direction.

"Honestly, I'd rather ignore him, pretend nothing is happening, and hope he goes away. Just in case it isn't courting behavior, and he figured out something else." Charlotte whisper-hissed the last part.

Cassie snorted and went back to admiring the dress in the mirror. "Okay, but it is right before your birthday. Perhaps he has a reason to follow you." She wiggled her eyebrows at Charlotte. "Maybe he wants to make sure no one else lays claim to you first?" She looked back at the mirror, then caught up with Charlotte's last statement. "Oh." She leaned in and whispered back. "You think he suspects you are a ... you know, and is trying to prove it? Or see if you turn?"

"I don't know, but that seems more likely than following me around for mating purposes. If that was the case, wouldn't he have started this earlier?"

Cassie laughed, but it was very strained. "I don't know. Maybe he senses you could be mates. And he either isn't sure or wants to figure out how best to approach you. He is older than you are, so would have already figured out the two of you are matched. It could be romantic, actually. He waited for years, and now you're so close to being able to mate, he can't leave you alone." Cassie let out a romantic sigh.

"Yeah, except this is Brian we're talking about. Womanizing, arrogant, bullied other kids in high school, Brian. I wouldn't hold my breath about him being concerned about what I want. Can you imagine?"

"Yeah, okay, I will admit, the 'trying to catch you doing ... things' does seem like a more likely answer. We will just have to keep an eye on him. Make sure he isn't trying to cause issues for you. He isn't the most tolerant guy."

Charlotte frowned at her cousin before looking back across the street. and was not surprised when Brian was gone.

"Well, he got out of here fast," Cassie commented as she peered around her mirror to glance out the front windows.

"Yeah, happened last time too."

– – – – – – – –

Two days later, Charlotte was off work and not ready to return to her parents' house, so she grabbed a paperback from the trunk and went out to sit in the gazebo in the middle of downtown. Charlotte was a big bookworm, carrying two or three books in her trunk at all times. Sure, she also had an e-reader, but she was always forgetting to charge it.

She grabbed a coffee from the little stand in the corner of the green space that held the gazebo and settled in. She briefly paused reading, drank some coffee, and sighed contentedly. There was Brian again, several yards away, frowning at her as if *she* was intruding on *his* time.

Charlotte was resolute to not look away and lose him again. Frowning, she narrowed her eyes at him and waited to see his next move. Brian looked at her thoughtfully for a moment, cocking his head to the side before he scowled. Brian crossed his arms and stared her down, clearly hoping she would look away first. Knowing it wasn't smart to stare him down, she did anyway. She would not cower because the alpha's son was following her around, probably trying to catch her doing magic.

Sure, Crescent Falls wasn't a big city, but she had seen him more times in the last three days than in the three months prior. It wasn't something she was about to ignore.

Brian took two gigantic steps towards her. Charlotte's heart sped up, but she didn't look away. She couldn't look away. He snarled at her before dropping his arms and striding in the opposite direction, across the park and down the street. Charlotte watched him until he was completely out of sight and then continued to watch the direction he had gone in for another few seconds.

She didn't know what was happening, but she didn't like it. Her gut told her to worry and be on-guard. A smaller, darker voice in the back of her head chimed in that he'd seen her performing some kind of magic and had more nefarious reasons for hunting her down. That thought had her hoping he was following her because they were mates. The idea Brian followed her because she could be a hybrid and would therefore need to be, the best-case scenario, run out of town was definitely not something positive that would come from her twenty-fifth birthday.

Charlotte tried to get back into her book; after another half an hour, she just couldn't concentrate on it. Her brain warring with itself just drew too much of her attention, so she gave up, went back to her car, and headed home.

Chapter 2

Charlotte

Every Friday, the alpha hosted a barbecue for the pack. No one was required to come. Nevertheless, most of the pack showed up. It was held no matter the weather; people could be in shorts and tank tops, or a heavy leather jacket and jeans. It was a way to create community. Though she really didn't want to come, Charlotte's mom had cajoled her into it, saying she was so close to her Wolf Moon, the term for the first full moon after a werewolf's twenty-fifth birthday that would lead to their first shift, it would be nice for her to have one last community outing as a juvenile.

Charlotte growled at the term 'juvenile' but went along because it would make her mom happy. Several of her friends, as well as half their family, were there. Charlotte enjoyed the first two hours with plenty of people to pal around with. Until she got a weird prickly feeling when she was talking to Cassie and one of their cousins, Muriel. Charlotte felt her shoulders bunch and was about to turn when Muriel muttered to her and Cassie.

"Don't look now, but Brian is smoldering at us or glaring daggers. I'm not sure which, since his face always looks like a cross between eating something sour and constipation."

Muriel spoke her mind and at twenty-six it wasn't exactly socially acceptable. Charlotte adored her for it.

With a huff, Cassie looked over Charlotte's shoulder. "Really, this again?!"

Muriel raised her eyebrows and turned her attention to Cassie. "What does that mean?"

Charlotte briefed her on the first two times she saw Brian this week and informed them both about the last time.

"Is he giving chase or hunting you?" Muriel's disgust was clear. "I mean, don't get me wrong, I enjoy a good chase but, if he hasn't talked with you about it first, it's creepy." She shifted her gaze to Charlotte, giving her a loving look. "Shall I chase him away for you?"

Charlotte snorted. Muriel was almost six feet tall and built like a fighter. But that still didn't mean it was in anyone's best interest for her to get into a fight with the alpha's son.

"Thank you, no. I am hoping he gets past whatever this is, and we can just pretend it didn't happen. I am not sure of his motives; a mating chase seems odd this long after his Wolf Moon. If he knew we were mates, wouldn't he have tried to at least be friends before now?"

Werewolves couldn't sense their mate until their Wolf Moon, after their first change, to be more specific. It didn't matter if the mate had gone through their Wolf Moon or not. The mate's scent would call to the werewolf meant to be their mate.

She'd heard it described as the smell of home. When she asked her mother about it, the response she got was there is a pull towards your mate. Their scent would be the most comforting smell in the world to you, whether you knew what that was ahead of time or not. It had the power to soothe an angry wolf and bring peace to an anxious mind.

"Healthy approach. Nothing ever goes wrong with that," Muriel retorted.

"I think it is more likely he suspects what I am."

Muriel's eyes widened a touch. "What, you think he is trying to out you? Char, that's not good. While kind to his own pack, Alpha Alexander is not exactly tolerant of outsiders. If he finds out, it will be a race to get you out of pack territory."

"You think I don't know that?"

"Whether it's healthy or not, it won't work. He's heading this way now," Cassie muttered.

Going wide-eyed, Charlotte spun to see Brian stalking towards them.

"Oh, come on!" Charlotte responded with an exhale.

"Don't worry, Char, Cass, and I will stand here with you. If things get hairy, we've got your back."

"Thanks, ladies."

Brian stopped just inside her bubble of personal space. From close range, she could tell Muriel was correct. His expression was intense, his chocolate brown eyes seemed to bore into her, but she couldn't tell whether it was supposed to be a smolder or a glare either. His blonde hair was pulled back in a tight ponytail, setting off his more angular features. It made the expression look harsher.

"Can I help you, Brian?" Charlotte mentally patted herself on the back for her calm tone.

"I'd like to talk to you for a few minutes, alone."

As he spoke, he wrapped his hand around her arm and tugged. As if that simple action would automatically make her give in.

"No, thank you. If you want to talk to me, you can talk to my cousins. You know how tight werewolf families are."

Now he was annoyed. "This is private." He over-enunciated the words through gritted teeth.

Muriel came to stand beside Charlotte, folding her arms across her ample chest. "No offense, Brian, but whatever you're about to tell her, she's turning around and telling us, so there's really no point. Privacy is an illusion."

Charlette noted the increasing number of eyes shifting in their direction.

Brian's gaze flickered to Muriel and then back to Charlotte. "I need to talk to you in private, now."

Even if she had been inclined to wander off with him, she certainly wouldn't do it with him snarling as much as he was. Without her wolf, she was at a distinct disadvantage, and she would not put herself in any kind of situation where she could be in danger.

"I said no, thank you; please let go of my arm."

Her tone was cool, though on the inside her heart rate picked up. He could easily drag her somewhere if he wanted to.

She was pretty sure her cousins, and by extension probably several other cousins, would follow.

"I don't have time for this." He started walking, tugging her hard. So much so, it caught her off balance, and she fell forward into him.

Before Charlotte could fully catch herself, she felt Muriel's arms around her waist, tugging her away, even though Brian still clutched her arm.

"Let go of my cousin. She said no." Muriel matched him with a growl of her own.

Charlotte had never been more grateful for her cousins.

"What's going on here?" came a thick, deep male voice.

Charlotte recognized it immediately. It was her oldest cousin, Riker. Riker was thirty-nine, six-and-a-half feet tall, and a huge wall of muscle. He'd played professional football until last year, when he retired. His werewolf genetics meant he wasn't slowing down like other men his age. He'd made the choice to retire before it became blatantly obvious there was something different about him.

"Brian is trying to drag Charlotte off for some privacy. She has told him no multiple times. He won't let go," Muriel summarized quickly before Brian could speak.

Riker folded his arms over his chest and frowned down at Brian. Riker was better at pack politics than Charlotte, Cassie, and Muriel. But he was also incredibly overprotective of everyone he deemed his, that included the twenty cousins he shared with Charlotte on her father's side. He might not outright challenge Brian, but he would walk that line better than anyone.

"Is that so? Is there a reason you're trying to take my cousin against her will?" Though his tone was neutral, his eyes burned.

At this point, they garnered a large audience. Brian was the alpha's first son, and women flocked to Riker both inside and outside of the pack.

Brian was outright snarling now. "This does not concern anyone but Charlotte and me. I would appreciate if you would stop making a scene and let her come with me so we can talk."

Riker slowly turned his gaze from Brian to Brian's hand on her arm, to Muriel's arms around her waist, to what Charlotte assumed was the unpleasant expression on her face.

"I am going to go out on a limb here and say she is what is stopping her from going with you, not any of us. And as long as my cousin does not want to go with you, she is not going with you."

Riker looked down at Charlotte for confirmation, and she gave a quick nod.

"See, there you go, so please let go of my cousin."

Whatever snapping remark Brian intended to make was interrupted when another voice boomed from behind him. "What is going on over here?"

This time, the voice belonged to the alpha. Which meant they could have a problem. If the alpha agreed Charlotte should go off with Brian alone, there would not be a lot the cousins could do to stop it without challenging the alpha outright.

Charlotte knew the second Riker came to the same conclusion because he stiffened and his eyes moved sharply past Brian, to where she assumed the alpha was walking toward them. At only five-foot-five, she couldn't see over the crowd as well as Riker could.

It only took a few seconds before the crowd parted and Alpha Alexander strode toward them. He took in the entire scene, quickly filing away little bits of information before stopping next to his son. He slid his hands in his pockets, clearly not trying to escalate the situation further by presenting a dominant or aggressive posture.

"Son, would you care to explain what's going on here?" His voice was calm.

"I need to speak with Charlotte alone. And her cousins will not let her leave." The way he said the word cousins made it sound like an insult.

Alpha Alexander lifted one eyebrow and then looked at each of them. His bright amber eyes settled on Charlotte.

Her heart rate picked up again. The smallest tendrils of fear began creeping in.

"As far as you're concerned, Charlotte, is that an accurate representation of events?"

"No," she answered softly.

He continued to watch her, encouraging Charlotte to continue without actually replying.

Taking a deep breath, she spoke slowly and quietly. Charlotte wanted to make it clear she wasn't trying to cause a scene, though she knew full well they now had the attention of every wolf within hearing range. Having that extra attention would only give more fuel to the fire if Brian was really trying to prove her secret. It would make him more determined that she was a problem.

"Brian walked up to us and said he wanted to talk to me alone. I said no thank you, and he grabbed my arm and tried to tug me away. My cousins intervened to stop him, since I clearly didn't want to go." Part of her wanted to tell him about how Brian kept popping up and staring at her all week. But she felt wasn't the right time to bring that up.

Alpha Alexander watched another second before turning back to Brian. "Let go of the girl. We do not take women against their will. We don't take anyone anywhere against their will unless there's some kind of conflict or safety issue. Is there some sort of safety issue at the party that you're not telling us about?" he asked calmly, as he raised his other eyebrow at his son.

Brian swiveled his attention to his father and snarled. "No, I just need to talk to her."

"I, as your alpha, think you need to let go of her and talk to me." Alpha Alexander threw a bit of power behind his voice. There was a certain level of dominance magic an alpha wolf had. Alexander used just a little against his son to enforce his will.

Brian let go and took a step back. Muriel, however, kept her arms around Charlotte's waist. She wouldn't let go until Brian was well enough away.

"Very well, Father, lead the way." Brian inclined his head to his father.

The alpha turned, and the crowd parted again as both blond men walked back into the pack house that served as a meeting place and headquarters for all pack events.

There were several moments where everyone just stared at each other quietly. Before anyone could corner them to ask for more information about the events, Riker turned to Muriel, Charlotte, and Cassie, leaning down more than a foot to whisper. "How about the four of us go somewhere a little quieter?" He pointed his head towards the tree line at the edge of the yard.

The three women nodded quickly, and Muriel slowly let go of Charlotte and led the way, with Riker taking up the rear, politely, discourage anyone from approaching.

Chapter 3

Charlotte

Once they got to the woods and clearly out of earshot, Riker dropped his hands and slid them into his back pockets.

"All right, Brian's always been a douchebag, but that was weird. Care to fill me in on what exactly is going on?"

Neither Cassie nor Muriel spoke. Charlotte let out a heavy sigh and filled Riker in on the whole situation. The further she got into the story, the more severe his frown became .

When she finished, he waited several beats. "I'm not gonna lie; I'm sincerely hoping this is not his mating behavior. I don't want to get into a fight with the alpha's son about his treatment of my cousin. But it would be infinitely worse if he found out you are possibly a hybrid. I wish there was a way to find out what his motives are. I don't think he'll tell me. But I don't like the two of you being alone, Charlotte."

An idea percolated in Charlotte's mind. "I could go listen in on their conversation."

"No!"

"Absolutely not!"

Muriel and Riker chimed in at once.

Charlotte frowned. "You both know I'm quieter and stealthier than pretty much anyone else, at least in our family, if not in the pack. If they find me, I'm headed to the bathroom. I would put money on them being in the alpha's office. Which is two doors down from the bathroom."

Charlotte started moving along the tree line back to the house before any of her cousins could say anything else. It wasn't the best idea, but wolves close to their Wolf Moon were known for being impulsive and a little moody.

Riker ate up the ground between them fast, and Charlotte was pretty sure he told the others to go back to the party.

"This is not a good idea, Charlotte."

"Maybe not, but it's the only one I've got and I am sick of being stalked."

Riker snorted. "All right, but at least let me be your lookout."

As they popped out of the tree line, Charlotte couldn't help but laugh. "Riker, I love you. You are one of my favorite cousins, which is saying something since there are a lot of them. But you are a bull in a china shop. I am not convinced you could sneak up on anyone or anything." She patted him on the arm and picked up the pace, taking the stairs to the deck two at a time.

She heard a growl behind her, but Riker stopped walking. He disagreed with her going alone, but knew she was right.

She nodded at the handful of people in the kitchen and continued walking, just like she would to the bathroom. But as she hit the main hallway, she slowed her steps, moving lightly and swiftly.

Charlotte crept down the hall, careful to stay on the side with the alpha's office so her shadow wouldn't give her away. She couldn't believe her luck. The door was ajar. That meant she could stand closer to the entry, out of scent range, and still hear their conversation, provided they didn't whisper.

"For the last time, Brian, what was so important you needed to drag that woman away from her family?" The alpha growled, clearly upset, but holding back his temper.

"I told you, it's nothing you need to worry about right now. I've just been monitoring her, and this was the first chance I had to talk to her."

There was the sound of furniture moving.

"Brian." The alpha's voice sounded exasperated. "Have you been stalking her? Or performing a mating hunt?"

Charlotte held her breath as the silence in the office continued. It went on for several long beats before there was some shuffling. Brian growled.

There was amusement in the alpha's voice now. "Is she even old enough to mate with you?"

Brian growled, and the alpha chuckled.

"Her birthday is coming up. Within the next moon cycle or two, she will be."

"Is she aware of the situation?" Alpha Alexander asked.

"No, but there are other bits of information I need before I decide how to move forward."

It felt as if ice flowed through her veins. He knew, or he suspected, she was a hybrid and was waiting to see if she changed. This was bad. The alpha might not have caught the disgust in the growl when their being mates was brought up, but she did.

The alpha took the silence as the answer he wanted.

"If you're not explaining the situation to her, I can understand why she would want nothing to do with you."

Charlotte didn't stick around to hear the rest of the conversation. There had always been a loose plan in place in case this very thing happened, and it would take a few days to get all the wheels in motion. She needed to start now. She had to run, had to get out of pack territory before she could be run out, or worse.

She moved swiftly and quietly down the hall. This time, the kitchen was blissfully empty. Charlotte took a deep, shaky breath before schooling her face and heading back outside.

Riker stood where she left him and scrutinized her face. From his expression, she figured she was not hiding her thoughts as well as she'd hoped.

"What's wrong?"

Charlotte steadied herself by looping her right arm through Riker's left. "Riker, I need you to take me home."

He searched her face. Then pulled his phone from his back pocket and nodded. "Of course, let me text Uncle Syler and let him know, so he doesn't try hunting you down later when he and Aunt Erica are ready to go."

She appreciated Riker's foresight about texting her dad. She had completely forgotten she'd carpooled with them.

"I'm also texting Muriel so she won't go looking for you. She'll get the word out to anybody else pertinent."

"Thank you, Riker. You know how much I appreciate and love you, right?" Charlotte whispered.

Riker smiled down at her as he slid his phone back in his pocket and turned them to walk around to the front of the house where the cars were parked.

"Of course, I do. I'm absolutely amazing. Who wouldn't love me?"

Charlotte snorted and gave a halfhearted laugh while squeezing his arm.

"I actually need one more thing. Will you text Dad 'pumpernickel'? He'll know what it means. "

The smile left his eyes. "I know what that means. He told me years ago. How much time do we have?"

"Until the full moon."

Riker nodded again, pulling out his phone and relaying her message. Once his phone was back in his pocket, he threw his arm over her shoulder and gave a squeeze. In the privacy of the truck, she replayed the conversation.

Once back at her parents', Riker followed her inside. They snuggled up on the couch. He turned on some music and stroked her hair comfortingly while she leaned on his shoulder.

After a half hour, he spoke. "You calling your Aunt Angela tonight or talking to her when she comes to your party tomorrow?

Her Aunt Angela was her mother's older sister. She was mated to a beta wolf two packs over from Crescent Falls. Angela was a bit of a free spirit, living on her own in the woods when she met Ferdinand, and he swept her off her feet. Being so far away, she was the first step in Charlotte's escape plan.

"Tomorrow is soon enough. Brian can't make a move until I shift, though it might be best having my Wolf Moon in Aunt Angela's home territory instead of here, just to be safe. I want one more night before everything blows up."

"Alright," Riker responded before kissing her on the forehead and they both lapsed back into silence.

Chapter 4

Present Day

Adam

Adam needed to decompress. He had been the alpha of the Valley River pack for ten years now, ever since his father died defending the pack from a group of rogues. Adam had been training to take over when the attack happened. It hadn't been until he finished fighting several rogues himself that he'd even noticed his father was wounded. He hadn't known how wounded until much later.

Even after doing this job for a decade, he still got incredibly irritated when he, as the pack alpha, had to deliberate over what he felt were unimportant issues.

"The summer solstice ball is important. Not only for our pack but for the relationships with the packs we invite," challenged Marcus, who did the party planning and guest relations for the pack.

"No one is questioning the importance of the ball. But we are in the middle of a security meeting and what you need to talk to Adam about can wait until we are done," snapped Ralph, one of Adam's two lieutenants.

They had been discussing a recent security breach. Some unknown wolves kept crossing into the Valley River pack's territory. They were spit-balling ideas of how to keep an eye out without making the pack too nervous when Marcus strode in, claiming there was an emergency with the ball. The solstice ball, which while a big deal, was one of four balls they threw each year, as the largest pack in the region. It also was three weeks off and Adam could not understand how there could be a party-related emergency this far out.

"What exactly is the problem, Marcus?" Adam asked, trying not to show his annoyance at the interruption.

"The witches of Dark Falls have declined your invitation. We just received word." Marcus was clearly panicked.

Adam understood the other man's panic. Witches were solitary, or met in small covens, but they had ruling bodies that divided up the world in four sectors. When one of these super covens made a ruling, every witch in that region would obey, or face harsh consequences. North America was presided over by the witches of Dark Falls in British Columbia. Even since before his grandfather's time, the witches sent representatives to both the winter and summer solstice balls to give a blessing to those in attendance. It was a gesture of goodwill and friendship, put in place to stop the two groups from continuously fighting and killing each other. The witches' absence from a ball would be a problem and might be seen as a break in a carefully written treaty.

"Did they say why they weren't coming?"

"No, they just sent back their invitation with the X next to decline," Marcus responded nervously.

"Okay, I can't address a problem I don't know about. Reach out to them and find out exactly why they're refusing to come. Maybe there is something we can do to help encourage them. But only if we know what the problem is. Can you do that, Marcus?"

The other man bobbed several times nervously before darting from the room.

Once the door was shut again, Vince, Adam's beta, leaned in to whisper in Adam's ear. "Well, that's probably not great."

Adam snorted at his beta's understatement.

Instead of replying, Adam turned to the room at large, to the four other men and one woman who made up the Security Council. "All right, the trespassers don't seem to have caused problems yet, but I'd rather not chance it. Let's double the patrols of our perimeters. I want us walking those perimeters day and night, twice what we're doing now. Maybe it's overkill and they're just passing through, but I don't want an attack like there was ten years ago."

Though Adam held back his own wince at the mention of his father's, several others at the table could not.

When no one said anything else, Adam stood. "All right, you're all dismissed."

As they began standing, Adam put his hand on Vince's shoulder. The black-haired man stayed put, easing into a more relaxed sitting position as everyone else filed out.

"Vince, I'm stepping out for the afternoon and going for a run. If anyone asks, I'm running errands and will be back tomorrow."

Vince wasn't just his beta, he was Adam's best friend since childhood. The son of his father's beta. They were raised to rule the pack together, and it was a bonus to be best friends.

Vince smiled up at Adam before standing and patted him on the shoulder, his eyes conveying sympathy. "Yeah, Adam, I'll cover for you. There is a lot going on right now and I'm sure it's bringing back a lot for you. Take the run while you can get it, because in another two weeks, you'll be entertaining dignitaries. And before that, you'll probably be groveling to witches."

Adam snorted. "Thanks, man."

Vince gave him a nod before striding out of the conference room.

Adam locked up his office for the day before heading home to drop everything off, so he could go for a very much-needed run.

Chapter 5

Adam

Pushing his wolf body as fast and as far as he could helped clear Adam's head. He'd started his run with two perimeter checks before leaving pack lands and heading into the neutral zone between Valley River's lands and their nearest neighbor, the Serenity Lake pack. Adam was on good terms with the Serenity Lake's alpha, Carson. Even if he ran through the neutral zone and into Serenity Lake territory, the older man wouldn't hold it against him. Knowing Carson, he'd probably invite Adam to the pack house for drinks.

Carson was his father's age, maybe a little younger, but took Adam under his wing, as best he could, when Adam's father died. He showed him the ropes and gave advice. Though Adam used that advice less and less as the years went on, the older man still held a special place in Adam's world.

If he got bored running the nine miles across the neutral zone, he might impose on the older man for some advice, or maybe that drink. Shaking his furry head, Adam put on more speed. If he could tire himself out, then his brain would clear of all these thoughts of intruders and why the witches would cancel for the first time in anyone's recollection.

Pushing his legs, Adam forced himself to clear his mind, concentrate on the surrounding woods, and run. It had been a long time since he let himself get absorbed in his wolf, and enjoy the sights and sounds of the forest, without some kind of ceremonial run or hunt. To just be himself.

– – – – – – – –

He continued for he didn't know how long. But when he finally slowed, when the anger, frustration, and bad memories finally cleared his head, Adam relaxed some. He'd sprinted all the way to the neutral zone that butted against Serenity Lake's territory, where there were miles and miles that backed onto a mountain range not claimed by any one pack. It was where alphas met if they needed neutral ground. There was a small group of independent wolves who ran a resort up on the mountain. Both humans and wolves were welcome, though the humans who occasionally made their way there only saw a moderate ski resort; several amenities where behind locked doors a human guest's keycard would never access.

Adam had not run like this since after his father died, those early years when he took on the mantle of alpha before he was ready. Back then, long painful, enduring runs had been the only thing that kept Adam sane.

A breeze picked up around him and a scent grabbed his attention; it smelled like honey and pastries. Much like his grandmother's kitchen when he was growing up and she would make cinnamon rolls for Christmas morning. But this didn't smell like food, this smell, was coming from a she-wolf.

Curious, he followed the scent. At first, he only found it when the breeze came through. But after the first few minutes it became more solid, he was coming closer to the source. The smell was pleasant and intoxicating. Adam had smelled nothing like it in his life. He wanted to roll in it. He wanted whatever that smell was.

After following the trail, he came upon a clearing and heard a woman humming to herself. Crouching down to an army crawl through the underbrush, Adam was careful not to make his presence known.

She was gorgeous, and when she pivoted in his direction, her sundress spun, and red hair whipped over her shoulder. It a gut punch and Adam immediately knew he was looking at his mate.

He inhaled her scent deeply, closing his eyes, savoring it, and committing it to memory. It was just like his sister had said—it smelled like home, like somewhere he could belong the rest of his life.

She was puttering around, behind a white picket fence, in an apron clearly too large for her.

He moved closer, knowing once she scented him their lives would change forever. The stress he dealt with would suddenly become bearable. She would open that little fence, run into his arms, and they would share that first mate's kiss. It would feel like fireworks. A confirmation for a mated pair.

Before he could do more than reach the tree line, a large pitbull came barreling out the front door to the cottage, barking, and snarling in his direction.

The beautiful woman straightened in panic, looked at the dog, then in the direction the dog was looking. Adam knew the moment she saw him, and he stepped further out into the clearing, donning a posture of friendliness.

The woman's eyes widened with panic, something he never would've expected. He tried to make himself look more friendly, wagging his tail, opening his mouth.

She dropped her trowel and faced him head on.

"Leave us alone, wolf. Whatever you want, we're not interested." Though her voice was stern, panic threaded through.

All Adam wanted to do was pull her to him, lay her head against his chest, and tell her everything would be fine. He wouldn't let anyone hurt her. Slowly he moved forward again, he was more than halfway across the clearing. But before he could start changing, she threw her hands out in front of her.

A second later, Adam was thrown back through the tree line and smacked into a bush. Shocked and slightly dazed, he continued to lie there a moment. He was sure the woman in front of him was a she-wolf. But he knew magic when he saw it, or in this case felt it.

His mate was a hybrid, the powerful, and hated mix of witches and werewolves. Now her solitary lifestyle made complete sense. She was hiding, from someone specifically or werewolf society as a whole, he didn't know. He would move heaven and Earth to remove anyone who would dare make his mate uncomfortable about her heritage. Just as soon as he could get within scent range.

Chapter 6

Adam

"I said leave us alone. Consider that a warning shot." Her voice told him she hadn't moved from where she'd stood earlier.

She knew he hadn't cowered and runaway.

Knowing he couldn't just give up on his mate now that he'd finally found her, Adam stood, and made sure there was no serious damage done from her spell.

He slowly exited the wood line again. He watched her eyes widen. As she splayed her hands to use another spell. He yipped at her, startling her enough to halt whatever spell she was about to throw.

She blinked at him, confused as he prostrated himself on the ground before whining pitifully, something he had never done in his entire life. If someone told him a half an hour ago, he would be doing this, he would've laughed at them. But now here he was, trying to get his mate's favor by seeming harmless.

He looked up at her continuing to whine, trying to make himself as small as possible, not an easy feat with his size, he then rolled over onto his back, displaying his stomach, something wolves don't do in front of a stranger. As he looked over at her, he could see how confused she was. She dropped her hand. Even her dog stopped barking.

Adam changed. Being an alpha wolf meant his change was much faster and more painless than most werewolves. But he purposefully made himself change slower, so as not to scare her.

When this change was complete, he knelt in the grass, sticking his hands in the air in surrender. During his change, she put her hands back up ready to throw a spell should she decide she needed to.

"Who are you and what the hell are you doing out here? Why can't you follow simple directions?" The last question was tacked on after a brief pause.

It made Adam grin.

"My name is Adam; I am from the Valley River pack. I was on a de-stressing run and strayed farther from my territory then I meant to." It wasn't exactly a lie. But something in him said telling her he was an alpha probably wasn't the best thing at the moment.

The woman frowned at him. "Stay where you are," she warned.

He nodded and continued to sit there, slowly lowering his hands to rest on his thighs. Though he was completely naked, he noticed she was being very careful not to look at him below the neck. Her modesty amused him.

He watched as she pulled out her phone and put it to her ear.

"Hello, Uncle."

She had the phone turned down low enough he couldn't quite make it out the other person.

"Honestly I don't know. How many people from the Valley River pack do you know?"

There was another long pause.

"One, or someone claiming to be one of them has shown up in my clearing. He got past the wards unscathed."

Adam had felt no magic wards as he followed her scent. Frankly, he was shocked he hadn't felt it. Based on her expression, the person on the other end didn't like that either.

"He says his name is Adam, says he's a member of that pack and was on a de-stressing run but seems to have overshot their boundary lines."

She tilted her head, frowning, continued to watch Adam for several seconds, appraising him, finally looking away from his shoulders.

"I'd say six-two, mid-thirties, black hair long enough he could tie it back if he wanted to, though there would be some of it in his face. Strong musculature but not like Riker."

Adam didn't know who this Riker was but instantly disliked the guy.

She met Adam's eyes again. "He wants to know if you can tell him what the alpha of Valley River keeps on his mantle that you wouldn't expect."

The question piqued Adam's interest. Who could she be talking to that would've seen the inside of his house? Most of his pack mates have been his house at one time or another. Her uncle was either a member of his pack, or somebody important enough to have been in Adam's private home instead of the pack house—another interesting development.

"He has a stuffed purple elephant on the left side of the mantle. It belongs to his little sister. She gave it to him a few years back when she left the pack to be with her mate, who is a wolf in the Serenity Lake pack."

He watched a little smile curl her lips. Adam wondered whether that pleasure was because he knew, or that he kept a token of his sister's, who he missed dearly, in his home. She relayed his answer to whoever was on the phone and waited a few beats.

"All right, thank you, Uncle. I promise I will check in with you in an hour and I love you too." She pulled the phone from her face before sliding it back into one of the many pockets in the apron.

"My uncle says with that tidbit of information you're likely a member of the Valley River pack. He's fairly certain he's met an Adam that fits your description. But Adam's a fairly common name."

She watched him a few more seconds, debating which question floating around her head she wanted to ask. Finally, she crossed her arms under a very generous chest and tilted her head at him.

"What exactly do you want, breaching my wards and coming up to the house?"

Adam knew to tread carefully. Whoever was on the other end of that call either had no idea who he was or knew Adam was the alpha and kept it from this woman. Or she was pretending not to know. She also had magic and lived in neutral territory alone. It was not the sort of situation he would've thought he'd find his mate in but definitely piqued his interest. Now probably was not the time to mention he was her mate. He wasn't entirely sure she would believe him.

"Curiosity mostly. To be honest, I didn't know I went through any wards, and I apologize for that. I didn't feel any. You might want to reset them. I was just running, heard you singing, so I came in this direction. I am sorry if I made you uncomfortable or afraid. I promise I was only out for a run." He tried to be as nonthreatening as possible.

"You're an awfully long way from your territory though. A good twenty miles, I think. Do you need help to get back?" She'd hesitated before asking.

He held up his hands and waved them. "No, no I'll be fine. I definitely ended up going farther than I thought I would. But if you could spare some water, I would appreciate it." He wanted an excuse for her to get closer to him. To smell him, to know the connection between the two of them. To know him for who he was, her mate.

"Oh, yes, of course." She spoke as if this was something she should've already expected. She turned away from him, letting that dress swing about her. And he got a better glimpse at her lush body as she turned and bent over.

"Here, catch," she called as she swiveled back around and much to his surprise, threw a water bottle at him.

"I haven't used it yet; I've been absorbed in what I'm doing so you don't have to worry about sharing germs or anything."

He smiled and murmured his thanks. Inwardly he winced, he hoped she would get closer, and she still hadn't even left her yard.

He took several sips before closing it and throwing it back towards her. She caught it before placing it down wherever she picked it up from and he was treated to another view of her backside, it was enough to make his imagination run wild.

"You have me at a bit of a disadvantage. You not only know my name but have seen me naked. Can I at least get yours?"

Her eyes went wide, and her cheeks flushed. "My naked?"

A genuine laugh bubbled up from his throat as he grinned at her. "No, your name."

Her pale face turned red with embarrassment. "Oh, yeah of course my name. Charlotte, the name's Charlotte."

She was adorable ... absolutely perfect. It was all Adam could do to hide the grin that creep onto his face.

"Wonderful to meet you, Charlotte. Can I ask what you're doing all the way out here by yourself?"

He cursed himself inwardly as she closes off again and stiffen, flexing her hands.

"I live out here." The words were cold and detached.

Adam held up his hands again. "I wasn't meaning to intrude. I was just curious."

She gave him a tight smile but didn't relax.

Knowing he needed to quit while he was ahead, even though it would hurt to leave her presence, Adam sighed.

"I hope you don't find me too rude, or too forward, but I really should get back since it's getting dark. But I was wondering if you'd be opposed to me visiting again?"

He was taking a gamble, this woman clearly didn't like visitors, but he didn't know what else to do.

She frowned, squinting, trying to decide if he was a threat to her.

"I can't stop you," she drawled. "But as long as you're not a threat to Buster or me, I won't blast you again if you enter the clearing."

Adam beamed; he couldn't help it. He'd found his mate. While their first meeting hadn't gone completely according to plan, she wasn't opposed to seeing him again, that is without smelling him. Once she did that, he was sure she would run into his arms.

Shaking his head clear, he prepared himself to start the change again. "It was interesting, and nice to meet you, Charlotte. Have a good however long it is until I see you again." With that, he changed back into a wolf.

Once he was on all fours, he lowered his front paws and bowed at her.

Amused, she rolled her eyes before turning back to her plants again. "Goodnight, Adam."

He trotted into the tree line, making sure to get far enough away neither she nor her dog would see him easily. He hunkered down and watched her putter around in her garden until some beeping noise startled her from inside and she ran in. Once it became dark, he huffed and began the long trek back to his territory.

Chapter 7

Charlotte

Charlotte wasn't surprised when her uncle Ferdinand knocked on her door at nine in the morning. She knew it was Ferdinand by Buster's reaction. Since she'd adopted Buster two years ago to be a companion, the young dog loved Ferdinand. If her uncle was around, Buster followed him and gazed up at him with a loving expression Charlotte never saw when the dog looked at her. For whatever reason, Buster's love for Ferdinand was unrelenting. Charlotte's aunt Angela joked that she would come home to see him cuddling on the couch with her husband one day.

With Buster whining at the door and his tail wagging so hard his butt wiggled, Charlotte couldn't help but smile as she yanked the door open to her uncle.

"Good morning, Uncle," she greeted.

She then backed out of the way so he could walk into the cottage her aunt once lived in. It was some distant relative's cottage before Angela inherited it, but since she was happy living with her husband in the Serenity Lake pack territory, the couple had been more than happy to let

Charlotte lived there after the weird kerfuffle with Brian.

They'd all expected him to show at her Wolf Moon ceremony and threaten her, which was why they ended up holding it out here at the cabin. But he hadn't appeared. Which meant her secret was safe, as long as she laid low. Though her family couldn't visit her in groups, and she had not been home in four years. She lived happily in neutral territory and worked for the resort up in the mountain, and occasionally with some local caterers. It wasn't a lot of money, but she was able to make a living.

Her uncle stepped in, giving Buster a gentle pat as the dog whined for the older man's attention. They both laughed; Charlotte shut the door and locked it again.

"Can I get you some coffee, Uncle?"

"That would be much appreciated, Charlotte," he answered in his gentle, melodious voice.

Before grabbing another mug, she popped a pod he liked into her Nespresso, then went about foaming some milk for him.

"Care to tell me about the visitor you had yesterday?"

"Fine, Uncle how are you? How is Aunt Angela? How are the twins? I haven't heard from them in quite some time. And you know when they're quiet, that's when things go sideways," she teased.

When she looked over, he rolled his eyes. "I just saw you two days ago, and we caught up completely. I wanted to make sure you're okay and that this visitor didn't try anything." He growled as he finished speaking.

She didn't blame him for his protectiveness. Her aunt Angela and her uncle Ferdinand were the wolves she interacted with most. She baked in her own kitchen, or the industrial kitchen she rented and the resort delivery werewolf, Henry, would come and pick things up.

Charlotte interacted with werewolves as little as possible. She didn't want Brian to find her. His anti-hybrid views would only be worse if he realized she'd lost some control over her magic once she gained the ability to shift into a wolf. She'd always been a gifted magic user, but even years later the power wasn't always there when she wanted it to be. She also wasn't the strongest wolf. As she got used to her shifts, Charlotte had to admit, many of her senses were not as strong as an average wolf.

As she set the hot latte in front of her uncle and began making one of her own, she sighed and walked him through her interaction with Adam yesterday. It wasn't until she was sitting down with her own drink and had taken those first few sips of a new cup that she finished.

Her uncle watched her warily, clearly processing the information. He was the beta to the Serenity Lake pack. Which meant he knew many people and was a very dominant werewolf. He didn't like situations he wasn't in control of.

"He wants to come back? Why?"

When she frowned at his curious expression, her uncle waved a hand dismissively at her.

"You are an incredibly lovely woman Charlotte, that is not what I meant. From what you've told me about the interaction, I don't understand why he would want to travel the twenty-two miles from his pack territory to sit naked outside your house and hold an awkward conversation." He continued frowning before shaking his head. "Either way, I am glad you're safe. And you need to fortify those wards." He lifted his coffee mug at her.

She mock saluted him. "Yes, sir."

He frowned again. "I mean it, kiddo, I don't like the idea that he didn't seem to notice the wards were there. Do you need me to hunt down some more spell books for you?"

Slowly, Charlotte shook her head. "Nah, I have plenty of them. I'm doing some work in the garden this morning, then I'm combing through the books again. I want to have this place re-warded before I have to leave for the city tomorrow to do some baking for the resort."

Her uncle nodded before downing the rest of his coffee. "Good, well I'll let you get to it. We look forward to seeing you for dinner on Wednesday." He raised an eyebrow in question.

"I missed it one time. I will be there this Wednesday."

Nodding he gave her an infectious grin. "Good, let me know if this Adam fellow shows up again. I love you, little one, be safe."

Charlotte stood with her uncle and walked him to the door. "Love you too, Uncle, hug my aunt for me."

"Will do." He wrapped her in a bear hug before heading back outside and around the back of her house where her car was parked. She was sure he'd parked next to her.

She heard the engine start up and the gravel spewing as he drove away. She had to admit the whole Adam situation was odd. But she was also equally curious about why her uncle was so interested.

Shaking her head, Charlotte set that aside. She had other, more pressing things to worry about. Like redoing all of her wards, which would take the better part of the day.

Chapter 8

Adam

"A representative from the Serenity Lake pack is here to see you," Vivian, the pack secretary, informed him after she knocked on his slightly ajar office door.

Curiosity piqued, Adam smiled at Vivian. "See them in."

He couldn't help but wonder whether one of their guards had seen him zigzagging across the property last night and Carson wanted to check on him. It wouldn't be the first time a guard reported to Carson that Adam had gone on an extra-long run.

Exhausted by the time he got home, Adam had crashed on his bed, not waking until his alarm went off in the morning.

It surprised him even more when Ferdinand, the Serenity Lake beta walked through his office door.

Vivian closed the door behind the beta, who for once, didn't bother to give Adam a polite smile as he strode across the office and stood on the other side of the desk. The older man's jaw clenched as he fought to not appear openly hostile towards an alpha.

Adam stood to echo him, not being one to sit when a visitor was standing.

"What's happened? Is Carson okay?"

Ferdinand frowned at him a moment before shaking his head. "Nothing has happened, Carson is fine, as far as I know. I'm here about my niece."

Adam stared at the other man, frowning for several seconds and then his brain clicked everything together and he cursed. "You are the uncle she called."

Ferdinand growled. Normally that would have been horribly insulting and something there might've been a fight over. While Adam had the urge to jump across his desk and fight the man over his disrespect, he didn't. The man in front of him did not know what was happening and was worried about his niece. Being growly made sense.

"What were you doing by my niece's cottage?"

Adam took a deep breath and gestured toward the closest of his two visitors' chairs. "You're going to want to sit for this."

The older man's frown deepened, but he sat in the chair. Adam followed suit, sitting in his office chair.

"Long story short, we have had some perimeter breaches recently. They have done nothing, yet, but I don't like the idea of unknown wolves in my territory. I went for a run, I went around our territory, then started with the neutral ground. I was halfheartedly seeing if I could find something. But mainly I was blowing off steam.

Then I smelled your niece on a breeze." He paused, hoping Ferdinand would get what he was implying.

The older man leaned forward, elbows on his knees, his eyes wide. "You smelled your mate." His tone held utter shock.

Adam nodded and leaned back in his chair. "I smelled my mate. I was quite surprised to find her, out in the middle of the woods, and on top of that, to be a witch."

He watched as the older man went pale. "You can't let anyone know she's out there, or that she's a witch. It's a well-kept family secret. It's for her protection." The older man's words were a whisper.

"So be it, if that's what's needed, then of course I'll do it. Even if I don't understand why it's a secret."

After a beat, Ferdinand leaned back in his chair and gave a strange chuckle. "Well, that explains why the wards didn't work. If you're her mate, that sort of magic will not work against you. Especially considering you mean her absolutely no harm."

A wary dread coiled through Adam stomach. "Does somebody else mean her harm?" He growled out the words as he watched the older man.

"Sort of, to be honest my understanding is the alpha's son in the pack she grew up in was stalking her. There is some debate amongst the family on whether he is her mate, or if he somehow found out she was a hybrid and wanted to punish her accordingly. About eighty percent of us think it is the latter." Ferdinand gave a long pause in his story where he looked Adam up and down curiously. "But with you as her mate, she might not have to hide anymore. An alpha like you would not tolerate old prejudices being thrown at his Luna."

Ferdinand raised an eyebrow at him, and Adam realized he had been growling.

"She is mine," he stated.

The older man opened and closed his mouth several times before running his hand through his thick black hair, clearly losing the fight to not smirk.

"Look, you mentioned people intruding in your territory. We've had that problem as well. It's the reason I had Charlotte put wards around her house. There are a lot of wolves, that don't seem to belong to a pack, that make their way that far into the woods and find her. And I am sure you know the prejudice against hybrids still runs strong in some circles. Since no one wants her hurt or word to get back to her home pack, we try to be as protective of her as possible. She has seen an uptick of things hitting her wards recently. I wonder if that's related to these wolves you're seeing."

Ferdinand stood and turned to walk out before turning back to Adam. "I won't tell her you are an alpha. But you should. She's understandably wary of alphas but, you've never, in all the years I've known you, given me any reason to think of you as anything other than honorable. If you're right, and the two of you mate, you're coming into a huge, ruckus family. You're going to need to impress a heckuva lot of people, so you should be prepared for that. My understanding is your family is relatively small.

We are loud and there's a lot of us." He smiled as he said that.

Adam could tell there was a lot of love in that family. Something he'd secretly yearned for since losing his father, and his mother died of a broken heart less than two years after. It had just been him and his sister, his parents were both only children so there were no aunts, uncles, or cousins to cushion the heartbreak. He'd always secretly hoped he would mate a wolf with a large family. Fate had smiled on him.

As Ferdinand turned back again, Adam scratched an itch that had been bothering him since last night. "Who's Riker? She said his name with a lot of affection." His lips ticked up into a snarl.

Genuinely surprised, Ferdinand laughed. "Oh, someone you'll have to worry about, but not in the way you think. Riker is the oldest grandchild. He is the oldest of the cousins, he's incredibly protective of the twenty-one grandchildren younger than him. He also has a bit of a soft spot for Charlotte. I think because she never does what he says simply because he said it. She isn't as in awe with him as a lot of the other cousins are. He would make a good alpha, if he ever became so inclined to challenge one for the position." Ferdinand smirked and gave a nod, before walking out of the room, shutting the door behind him.

So, his magical mate was the niece of a beta, that was interesting enough, but now there was another male who paid attention to her, and not for good reasons. He needed more information, and he needed to acquire it stealthily, which wouldn't be easy on top of having to deal with security issues and the ball.

A shrill chime let Adam know he had a text message.

He looked down, surprised to see the text was from Ferdinand.

Next time you want to go see her, just park your car at my house. We're a heck of a lot closer than twenty miles. Give yourself a break. And it means you can spend more time with her. You're welcome.

There was an address below that. It made Adam smile. Her uncle was going to help him, even a little. With a predatory grin, Adam forced himself to continue working. The sooner he could get work done, the sooner he could make his way out to his mate's cabin. Maybe even this time to get past the fence.

Chapter 9

Charlotte

It had been a very productive day in the industrial kitchen. Charlotte had not only gotten the order done for the wolves up at the lodge, but a dessert order for a local catering company, a human catering company, as well. Being a werewolf meant being able to move much faster than a human baker would, and it came in handy as she completed the orders.

When she returned home late afternoon, Charlotte made herself a simple salad for dinner, using vegetables from her own garden, one of her absolute favorite things in the world, then she itched to continued baking. She wasn't sure why after a day as busy as it had been, but she rolled with it. So instead of zoning out or reading her current mystery novel, she went about experimenting in the kitchen. She had been on and off trying to perfect a kind of stuffed cinnamon roll. Something gooier than a classic cinnamon roll. She wanted to make a double wall, stuffing icing between the layers.

She pulled the thicker, piped cinnamon rolls out of the oven just as Buster started barking. Panic rocketed through her; Buster was giving a warning bark, meaning someone was on their property. A second later, she turned her head to see him leaping out his dog door.

When she looked out the window over the sink in the kitchen, Charlotte frowned as she saw the same salt and pepper wolf from yesterday.

"Adam?" she shouted, knowing with his werewolf hearing he'd be able to hear her from where he sat outside the window, wagging his tail as he watched her.

He let out his own yip of a bark, letting her know he heard her and was confirming her suspicion.

Frowning, she swore there was a pile of clothes on the ground next to him. He'd come prepared to shift this time. While she'd expected him to show up again, she hadn't expected him back so soon. Part of her was flattered, but more of her was wary.

Wiping her hands on her cartoon dog apron, she headed out the front door and into the front garden. The white picket fence went all the way around the house; in the back it went a little higher, making it difficult, but not impossible, for Buster to break out. The fence had extra wards on it and wouldn't let anyone pass without her express permission, unless they were a welcome return visitor.

When she stepped outside, Adam had already shifted and was buttoning a pair of jeans. He looked over at her with a huge wolfish grin.

"Good evening, Charlotte." His voice was cheery.

She blushed—Adam was incredibly attractive. She wasn't entirely sure he wasn't showing off his well-muscled chest on purpose.

"Good evening, Adam, what brings you all the way out here so soon? Are you stress running again?"

"Not really, I just felt like seeing you."

Her heart beat a little faster. She hadn't had a man flirt with her since she became a werewolf. She'd gone out of her way not to socialize with anyone outside of the family, and Henry the delivery driver.

Her second thought though, she couldn't help but wonder if he was a spy. She knew it was paranoid and probably silly, but what if this man told Brian where she was?

"I didn't mean to upset you. I can go if I'm interrupting something." Adam's voice was unsure.

Charlotte realized she was frowning, her face giving away the nature of her thoughts.

She forced a smile and shook her head. "No, it's fine, I was just thinking about something." It was unlikely he was some kind of spy. But if he was, she certainly didn't want to give away her suspicions.

The huge smile was back, and he moved forward to lean on her fence. It was odd that the wards were not zapping him with electricity like they would anyone else. She made a mental note to check them later. Because when she'd checked the wards to her house this morning, they had been fine. She'd reinforced them just to be safe. Either this man was immune, or her magic was on the fritz. Charlotte found she couldn't be pleased with either of those options.

"I was hoping we could have a conversation; I'd like to get to know you better."

"Why?" Her tone was clipped, she knew the question was rude, but she couldn't help her suspicious nature.

His grin faltered slightly, but he forced it wide again. "I need a reason to want to get to know a beautiful she-wolf I stumbled upon in the woods?"

He lowered his voice to a deep rumble, one Charlotte felt in her stomach. Adam was sexy, drawing her in if she was honest with herself. And that low growl did things to her system. If she had been anyone else, she would've adored getting to know him. Her uncle let her know he was safe, but she could never be too careful. Especially since this man knew she was a hybrid.

"If you'd rather not, that's fine. I'd never want to put you in a position where you're uncomfortable."

Charlotte bit her lip in indecision. Buster jolted her from her thoughts by bumping into her leg. She hadn't noticed when he stopped barking.

"I'll tell you what," she said on a whim. "You can be my taste tester. I'm trying to perfect a new recipe. And I need an unbiased opinion."

Before she could stop herself or change her mind, Charlotte turned around and headed back into the kitchen to grab one of the new cinnamon rolls for Adam to try. It was silly to spend more time with this man, as attractive as he was. It was also bizarre she found him so attractive in the first place. In the years since she'd left Crescent Falls, she hadn't found any male this attractive. There was a pull to him that made her want to hop the fence and rub up against him.

The idea of Adam being a spy would hurt, but her uncle had vouched for him. Still, she wouldn't let slip where her home pack was. Pushing all that aside, Charlotte took a plate of cinnamon rolls to the garden.

Chapter 10

Adam

His mate was breathtakingly gorgeous, and absolutely adorable, a kind spirit. He watched as she warred with herself on whether to make him leave. And it pleased him to know she seemed to decide he could stick around. But then she said something about a taste test and scurried into the house.

Not wanting to make her uncomfortable, he waited patiently at the fence. He inhaled deeply and wrapped the smell of her around him. He couldn't wait until he could bury his face in her neck. Inhaling her scent would be both erotic and calming, Adam planned on doing it for the rest of their lives ... as soon as he could convince her they belonged together.

He smelled cinnamon, and pastry a few moments before she reappeared. The dog she called Buster stayed in the garden, staring at him the whole time she was gone.

The plate held two plump cinnamon rolls and Adam's mouth watered at the smell. He wasn't entirely sure if that was the cinnamon rolls themselves or her scent mingled with them.

"Okay, I'll give you one on a plate. With a fork. That way you don't get your hands sticky. Then I want to hear what you think. Give me your absolute honest opinion because I cannot make improvements if I do not know what's wrong."

The sentiment so echoed his own, when it came to the witches, Adam was startled.

He watched as she used a fork to transfer a roll to a plate stacked under the one holding everything. She then walked to the fence and Adam held his breath, waiting for her to scent him, to know he was her home.

He growled when after two steps, a gust of wind blew past her, towards him, sending her waves of red hair into her face. He was now downwind of her and hair covering her nose. If she had a particularly strong sense of smell, she would still be able to smell him, but an average werewolf wouldn't.

He grabbed the plate as she reached him and much to his chagrin, she backed up again to the middle of her walkway, well out of normal scent range.

"What are the odds," he muttered to himself.

"Odds of what?" Charlotte asked, tilting her head at him as she began forking the plump cinnamon roll.

Adam blinked, trying to come up with a reason for his remark. Her sense of smell might not be great but apparently her hearing was.

"I love cinnamon rolls." It wasn't a lie, just not the whole truth.

"Oh good, that works out even better." She then put a forkful of the cinnamon roll in her mouth and groaned.

Adam fought not to lunge over the fence. His wolf stirred within him, its attention drawn to his mate. The sound she'd made had Adam thinking of many scenarios he could create to hear it again. Most with them naked and him touching her. None involved cinnamon rolls.

"Try it, I promise they're not poisoned," she cajoled, motioning her fork to his plate.

Relieved, she misjudged why he wasn't eating, Adam smiled and took a forkful of the cinnamon roll on his plate.

It was delicious. More cinnamon-sugar flavor than he expected; also more icing, without it being overpowering. It was gooey without seeming undercooked.

"This is amazing." Adam was a little embarrassed at the disbelief in his voice.

The thousand-watt smile she graced him with knocked the breath out of him.

"Thank you, I've been trying to perfect exactly how to make it. I'm thinking these might do better as small cinnamon rolls instead of regular sized ones."

"I can't help you there, I think this is delicious the way it is."

She giggled—honest-to-goodness giggled—as she put another forkful in her mouth.

She was hypnotizing him, without meaning to. If she actually put effort into seducing him, Adam would be a goner.

They ate in silence for a few minutes while Adam tried to pull himself together.

"So, are you a baker? Or is this for a party?" He hoped since she was in such a good mood, he might be able to pry a bit more information out of her.

Smiling at him, she held up her hand over her mouth and spoke louder to be heard around it. "I'm a baker, I send sweets up the mountain to the lodge. I also work with a couple local catering companies. I wanted to have this perfected in time for fall and winter seasons. Something warm and comforting to have on the menu. But in order to have it perfected by fall, I have to work on it now. What do you do?"

Adam was pleased to get information out of her, he was even more pleased she wanted information about him. He puffed out his chest a little.

"I work in the government of my pack."

He watched her frown, though it wasn't as closed off as when he asked about her living arrangements yesterday. Just the same, Adam held his breath.

"Pack politics can be exhausting. I don't envy your job."

Instead of responding, as he was not sure now was the time to give his title away, Adam took another forkful. His mate was a fantastic baker.

"I've never had anything like this. It is delicious."

She seemed to blush further. "Thank you."

"No, thank you, I would travel out here to be your taste tester any day." What he wanted to say was that he could not wait to be her tester for the rest of their lives. Sitting in their kitchen together, sharing food.

Before he could come up with another topic, he felt his phone ringing from the back pocket of his jeans. Juggling the plate, he took his phone out and frowned when he saw it was Vince.

"Please excuse me, Charlotte, I have to take this." He took several steps away and answered the call.

"What's going on?"

"How long will it take you to get back here? We had another breach," Vince responded.

Cursing, Adam walked right over to Charlotte's garden, motioning with his plate as he set it down on the rhododendron bush against the fence.

"Half an hour, maybe. Assemble the guards, start going over the game plan and I'll get there as soon as I can."

He ended the call and looked over at Charlotte's worried face.

"Would you like me to call my uncle to help you? He's the beta of the Serenity Lake pack."

Adam was touched his mate wanted to help, even though she didn't fully understand the situation.

"Don't worry, you don't need to bother him." He waved and began walking away. Before he left the little clearing, he turned around and cocked his head to look at her. "We are having a ball to celebrate the solstice. Would you be interested in attending? It's in a little over a month."

Charlotte's eyes widened in surprise. "Oh, I don't, I ... I don't know. I don't know what day or time or any of that."

It was too good to be true to hope she would agree right away. But he had plenty of time to convince her. If she wasn't sure they were mates by then, one night at the dance would convince her.

"I'll bring an invitation with me next time I come."

Her eyes got a little lighter and her cheeks flushed further. "Okay, yeah. Stay safe, Adam, okay?"

He couldn't help but grin at her concern for him before he waved again and sprinted towards his car.

Chapter 11

Four days later

Charlotte

It had been four days since she last saw Adam. And though she was embarrassed to admit it, even to herself, Charlotte missed him. She'd only seen him twice. But part of her expected to see him the next night. The idea of him being at her house three nights in a row was silly, especially considering something happened with his pack. But four nights seemed a long time. Charlotte kept chastising herself every time he popped in her head.

She had been so distracted while speaking to Riker on the phone last night he demanded he swing by and take her out to dinner the following night. So here she was, linked arm in arm with Riker, walking down the main street of Serenity Valley, the human city between the Serenity Lake pack territory, and the Valley River territory. It was larger than Crescent Falls and several neighboring cities. It was easier for them to get lost in a crowd.

"So, are you going to tell me what has you in a funk yet, little cuz?" Riker teased.

There was no way Charlotte was going to tell Riker the truth. Not only was it pathetic, but he would tease her about it mercilessly and she didn't want to have to deal with that for what would probably be the rest of their lives.

"Nope, you want to tell me why we've passed several groups of werewolves inclining their heads to you, instead of just the usual 'hey, there is a celebrity' stares?"

Riker had played in the NFL, retiring last season. His caring nature made him a fan favorite. But the looks she was seeing from werewolves tonight were of deference, not just sideways glances and open gawks of football fans.

He shifted uncomfortably on her arm. "Yeah, about that. I was officially named the next in line for the Crescent Falls alpha this week."

Charlotte tripped on nothing but caught herself and stopped to gawk up at her cousin. "Hold the phone, what? Why didn't you open with that?" Her eyes couldn't get any wider.

Riker blushed in embarrassment and rubbed the back of his neck with his free hand. "You remember how about two years ago Brian disappeared and no one could figure out where he went or why?"

"Yeah." Even though he had been gone, she didn't know if he would return, or what he'd told alpha Alexander about her.

Riker eyed her warily. "Well, it turns out his father kicked him out. Alpha Alexander told him if he could not put the pack's needs above his own, and stop being ridiculous and selfish, then he had no business becoming an alpha. I don't know the details, but that was the gist of what Alexander told me."

"Whoa, are you serious? He kicked his own son and heir out of the pack?"

"Yes, and he has been sort of testing his two younger sons over the last two years to see if either of them is alpha material. He didn't want to make the same mistake again of just assuming one of them could do it. He apparently came to the conclusion a few months ago that neither of them would make a good alpha. So, he decided to send out feelers, and see who within the pack could be the better choice. There was a short list of three of us and we were unknowingly tested. I ended up on top. And Alpha Alexander approached me about it two weeks ago. It became official this Monday."

It was almost too much information. Charlotte's brain couldn't process it all. It was one thing to believe Brian was skulking around the pack not doing his alpha duties. But if Alpha Alexander kicked him out of the pack, then he couldn't be on pack lands at all. And her cousin was now in line to be alpha, someone not of the alpha's lineage. It wasn't unheard of, but it was an uncommon practice.

"Are you saying if I'm careful, I could go home? Because he wouldn't make you his successor if he knew what I was." Her voice was so quiet that if Riker hadn't been a werewolf, he wouldn't have heard the words.

He looked down at her with a kind and sorrowful smile. "Yes, if that's what you want. You can even stay in my extra bedroom until you're back on your feet, unless you want to move back in with your parents, that is. I poked a little, and it appears Brian did not share his suspicions with his father."

Her head was whirling. If Brian had been kicked out two years ago, she could've gone home two years ago. Charlotte wasn't even sure if she wanted to go home. She liked her life, though she did feel a little alienated. She could not get television, most radio, or the Internet, out in the neutral areas. It would be nice to have those things again.

"That's a lot," she whispered.

Riker squeezed her arm and began moving the two of them towards the restaurant. "It is, and we can talk about it or not talk about it. Whatever you want. And it's not as if you only have a certain amount of time to make this choice. I'm sorry I couldn't come to you at the time and let you know Brian had been exiled from the pack. I didn't know he hadn't left of his own free will."

She knew Riker meant it. He would've convinced her to come back two years ago.

"I need to think about it."

"You do that, let me know when you have an answer." He squeezed her arm and smiled down at her as they headed to the seafood restaurant they frequented when in Serenity Valley.

There appeared to be a wait, like most Fridays and Saturdays. Charlotte stayed outside as Riker ducked in to get added to the waitlist. She had not been out there more than a minute or two before she heard her name.

"Charlotte?"

She wasn't normally recognized in the city, unless it was by Henry, when he made deliveries, or by her family should they happen by. She certainly hadn't expected who she saw when she turned.

Adam strode towards her, clearly with a male and female couple, even though he was strides ahead of them. The woman looked slightly amused as Adam pulled away.

"What are you doing all the way out here?" Adam asked as he got closer, scanning the surrounding street.

"Planning to eat dinner," she answered slowly. "I assume you're here to do the same?"

The woman behind him snorted and covered her mouth to hide a laugh.

Adam frowned over his shoulder.

His movement caught her attention. Not the movement itself but it made his scent waft over to her, It was rain and moss, like when she opened the windows to her cottage after a storm. It was one of her favorite smells in the world. Though her sense of smell wasn't as good as most werewolves, Adam was standing close enough there was no denying the enthralling scent came from him. She wondered what soap or cologne he used. She couldn't imagine his natural scent being that mind-altering.

"Adam, are you going to be rude or are you going to introduce us to your friend?" chided the woman behind him.

Adam stiffened and Charlotte watched several emotions glide across his face. They were too fast for her to identify before he pivoted to face all three of them at once. Before he could do more than open his mouth, Riker came to stand beside her, dropping his arm over Charlotte's shoulders in a clearly possessive gesture.

Adam stiffened, then eyed Riker as if he was sizing up her cousin for a fight.

"Alpha Adam, to what do we owe the pleasure?" Riker asked, clearly ignoring the glare he was getting from Adam.

"Alpha?" The word was passed Charlotte's lips before she even registered what she was saying.

Adam's discomfort seemed to grow, and Charlotte was pretty sure she heard him growl.

"Ava, Sam, this is Charlotte, niece to the beta of the Serenity Lake pack. And Riker, the next in line to be alpha of Crescent Falls."

He was introducing them through gritted teeth, and Charlotte wondered if he was embarrassed to be introducing her to people. That thought caused a pang in her chest. She didn't know Adam, his reluctance to introduce her shouldn't affect her at all. But it did. And he hadn't told her about being in alpha. It hadn't exactly come up in conversation, but it seemed weird he hadn't mentioned it. Alphas were usually pretty confident and cocky about their status within the pack.

"It's nice to meet you, Ava and Sam. How do you know Alpha Adam?" That was Riker, diplomatic to the end.

Ava grinned at both of them before frowning at Adam. "Adam's my big brother. Sam is my mate, so he's kind of stuck with both of us. He's been bogged down with pack business, so we dragged him out for dinner off the pack lands."

"I'm doing the same thing for my cousin here," Riker laughed. "Just as a heads-up, this place." He jerked a thumb to the seafood restaurant behind them. "Has currently got a forty-minute wait."

"Thanks, man," Sam added, giving Riker a large smile. "We're actually headed to the Chinese food place down the block. But it was nice running into and meeting you both."

Riker exchanged nods with them, and they both stepped out of the way so the threesome could keep walking.

"All right, cuz, I'm going to need to know how you are associated with the alpha of Valley River." Riker raised an eyebrow as he spoke.

Charlotte let out a heavy sigh. "He was running through the woods and happened upon my cottage, twice. We held minimum conversations both times. It's just a shock to see him anywhere else."

Riker frowned, all teasing leaving his face. "He made it through your wards, twice?" He said the word 'wards' as quietly as possible.

"Yes, and before you ask, I double checked them both times. And they seem to be in working order."

Riker looked up and watched in the direction the threesome had left. "That's odd. Maybe it's a sign you need to come home to us." He smiled down at her. Though it didn't quite reach his eyes.

Rolling her eyes, Charlotte patted his arm. "I said I'll think about it, and I will. Don't push it."

Riker gave her shoulders a squeeze and gave her a quick kiss on the top of her head. "All right, all right. Tell me about this top-secret thing you've been working on instead then."

"Oh no, you're not getting off that easy. I want to hear about you being next in line for alpha. Now that I'm apparently the last person to find out about it?" She gave him a stern expression, though there was no real heat behind it.

"All right, all right. You win. It all started two weeks ago..."

Chapter 12

Adam

"What on earth was that, you freaking weirdo?" Ava asked as she slapped Adam's arm once they were a block away from Charlotte and her cousin.

Adam shouldn't be surprised that her Riker was the Riker he met in a meeting yesterday. But he was. He also wasn't looking forward to apologizing for not telling her he was an alpha. It had not come up in their conversations but knowing they were mated, it felt like a lie, and like something he shouldn't have kept from her. He felt horrible.

"What was what? I met Riker yesterday, since he officially became next in line for his pack's alpha," he responded.

"No." She smacked him again. "Your weird reaction to the woman, Charlotte. I have not seen you be weird like that in years. It was uncomfortable, and I was just witnessing it. Right, Sam?" She looked over her shoulder at her mate, who was now walking half a pace behind them.

"Oh no. Do not involve me in this," Sam responded from behind them on a chuckle.

"I always liked you, Sam," Adam responded.

There was another chuckle.

"You did not, you threatened to castrate him like three times. But don't change the subject, I want to know about Charlotte." She used extra emphasis on Charlotte's name, trying to get a rise out of him.

"She's a wolf I've met a couple of times now and had passing conversations with. It wasn't in town, so I was surprised to see her out and about."

There was another smack against his arm. "You liar, liar, pants on fire," his sister practically shrieked. "You like her. I could tell by the way you were acting. And the defensiveness when her cousin slung his arm around her shoulders. You wanted to punch him in the face repeatedly."

Adam gritted his teeth. He did not want to be having this discussion with his sister. "Just drop it, Ava."

"Nope." She was skipping next to him now. Then without warning she froze and gaped at him. "Is Charlotte your mate? Did we just meet your mate?" Her voice was filled with disbelief, and she reached out and shook his arm, forcing him to stop walking as well.

Adam slowly turned to look at his sister, giving her the best glower he could manage.

"Oh my gosh, she is. Sam!" Still holding Adam's arm, Ava made eye contact with her mate. "I'm right, that was Adam's mate. My big brother finally met his mate!" she said louder than Adam would've liked.

"Keep your voice down, Ava," Adam growled.

His sister only giggled in response. "Why didn't you introduce her as such?" She was still holding his arm, preventing him from moving.

With a huff he pivoted to look at her. "She doesn't know yet, for whatever reason any time I'm near her I seem to be downwind. So, while I am one-hundred percent positive she is my mate. She thinks I am just some guy that keeps showing up. She is wary because apparently the alpha's son from her childhood pack was stalking her." While he would tell them that, he knew Charlotte wouldn't appreciate him telling them why.

His sister's expression fell apart and Adam hated taking the smile off her face. But he wanted to rip off the bandage before his sister went skipping back to where Charlotte and Riker stood and began talking to her as if they were sisters.

"Do you know his name?" Sam asked with interest.

Adam was surprised to realize that he didn't. He assumed once he had the time, he would research the other man. But he wouldn't have been able to even if he had the time.

"No, actually."

"It's a bit slow at work right now. Do you want me to do some digging for you?" Sam asked.

"No, that's okay, I really want to do it myself." As much as Adam wanted the help, she was his mate. He wasn't sure he could handle someone else poking around in her business, even if that other person was his sister's mate.

Sam shrugged. "Suit yourself." With that he moved around Adam and began walking towards the restaurant they planned to have dinner in.

Before following Sam, Ava launched herself at Adam in a quick, tight hug. "I'm sorry, Adam, let me know if there's anything I can do, okay?"

Adam rubbed his little sister's back. "Sure, Ava, I will." Even though he had absolutely no intention to do so. Any problems he and Charlotte had were between them. He wasn't involving anyone else.

Chapter 13

Adam

It had taken Adam the better part of the day to get a hold of and talk to a representative of the witches. It turned out they'd heard rumblings of several packs in the area having rogues in their territories, and the witches decided it wouldn't be safe to send representatives to the ball. Especially if the packs were overthrown—they did not want to appear to be taking sides.

Adam gritted his teeth through the phone call but promised whoever came would have a security detail of their own, and he would have backup vehicles available to them should they need. It wasn't the best-case scenario, but it was all he could think of, considering they still didn't have a lead on these rogue wolves. He tried to be as diplomatic as possible when he pointed out they attended the balls in years past and breaking the routine now could be seen as them picking a side.

Eventually, the representative relented and agreed to send three witches to give the solstice blessing. Adam waited until he was off the call to give a sigh of relief. Not having the witches to give the blessing would have looked bad, not just on him and his pack but on the general region. He didn't need to give the rogue wolves more legitimacy by having a long time, sort-of ally disappear on them during one of the year's most important events.

Adam let Marcus know; the other wolf was relieved. Then, as fast as he could, he made his rounds and cut out of the pack office as soon as wouldn't have been noticeable. He hadn't seen Charlotte since running into her downtown. He wanted to check in with her. They had been close enough she should've smelled his scent, gotten that pang of home. He wasn't sure whether the revelation that he was an alpha had been enough to throw her off, or if she was ignoring it entirely. Either way, he wanted to give her a ball invitation and apologize for keeping his identity a secret. It wasn't the best way to start a relationship with his mate, but he had hoped they would get to know each other better on a more even playing field. Now the cat was out of the bag, and he needed to make the most of it.

– – – – – – – –

Adam smiled as he got closer to Charlotte's cabin. He stopped by a florist, on a whim, thinking she might appreciate a bouquet for that little kitchen of hers. Maybe, this time he'd be allowed inside the house. Or at least inside the gate. As he got closer, he started to hear sounds of a fight.

Worry and adrenaline shot through him as he began to run, still in his human form, towards the cabin. Buster was barking frantically. Adam stopped just outside the clearing to take in the scene. Three wolves were in a standoff. As quickly as he could, Adam stripped off his jeans, shoes, and shirt, dropping the flowers and changing into his wolf. Once his wolf form snapped into place around him, he charged into the clearing, breathing deeply and was surprised the all-white wolf was Charlotte. White wolves were rare in this part of the country.

He ran up beside her and proceeded to growl at the two male wolves facing off against her. One more, this one all black, pulled out of the trees behind him and Charlotte.

Adam got her attention and moved his head to the newcomer. Charlotte did the dog equivalent of a nod before turning around to give her attention to the black wolf while Adam faced off against the other two. Pride overshadowed his feeling of worry at his mates' willingness to trust him at her back.

He growled and set his stance for a fight against the two wolves. Being an alpha and someone who'd been training to fight since a young age, he was confident he could take these two wolves with little problem. Knowing they posed a threat to his mate, he didn't even try to negotiate. While the two of them stood there trying to figure out what was going on, he leapt upon the first one and took advantage of the surprise to throttle the other wolf's neck. He ripped hard enough to incapacitate the wolf, though not enough to kill it. Before he could make the decision to do so, the second wolf clamped down on one of Adam's back legs.

Knowing a bite like that can do an awful lot of damage, he let go of the first wolf's neck, as the wolf dropped to the ground. The momentum of the drop meant the second wolf lost his grip momentarily, but the fangs slid up Adam's leg, searing pain following them; the giant gashes wouldn't heal for at least a week. Snarling, he turned and snapped at the other wolf. The two of them tumbled, falling into each other, each snapping, snarling, trying to get ahead.

Vaguely, he heard the noise of a fight behind him, and all Adam could do was hope Charlotte was holding her own.

After several minutes of swiping and snarling, Adam was finally able to grab one wolf's front legs and crunched down on the bone. The wolf screeched in pain and stopped trying to fight Adam.

Adam watched as he ran on three legs, into the woods, escaping to who-knew-where. His gut reaction was to go after the werewolf, to make him pay for attacking Adam's mate. But he didn't know how Charlotte was faring and wouldn't leave her alone with two potential threats. He pivoted to see Charlotte on top of the other wolf, biting down on the scruff at the back of its neck. Adam wasn't sure what exactly he was seeing, but the smell of magic—heavy magic, as light magic tends to not leave a scent— permeated the air. As he watched, the black wolf fell further to the ground and appeared to be unconscious.

Charlotte held on a few more seconds, making sure the black wolf was unconscious, before letting go and stepping away from the all-black wolf. Her attention swung to Adam. Once she realized who she was looking at, she breathed a sigh of relief. She gave him a look he didn't quite understand before she turned and took a running leap over her white fence and scampered into the house.

Assuming she was going in to change and wanted a little privacy, Adam moved into the woods where his clothes lay, unwilling to take his gaze off the two unconscious wolves in front of her cabin.

Once he'd changed, put his clothes back on, and grabbed the slightly dinged up bouquet, Adam headed back to the clearing to stand in front of the gate, pulling out his phone to call Vince. He could hear Charlotte speaking quietly, inside the house, probably making a similar call to her uncle.

"What's going on, boss?" Vince asked, his casual indicating he wasn't in the pack house anymore.

"Long story short, I got into a fight with what I'm pretty sure are some lone wolves in the neutral territory. I'm going to let Serenity Lake take care of them, but I wanted to let you know, as one of them got away."

There was silence a moment before he heard movement in the background on Vince's end of the phone. "Do you need assistance, boss?"

"No, it's all taken care of. I wanted you to be up-to-date. I'll let you know what Serenity Lake does with them."

"All right, you'll explain to me what you're doing in the neutral territory later, right?"

Adam winced; he hadn't told Vince he found his mate, or that she was living on her own in neutral territory. He needed to tell his beta soon, because there was no way he was leaving Charlotte in the woods by herself. She was coming to stay with him until they could neutralize this threat, whether she came willingly, or he threw her over his shoulder and dragged her into his territory.

Chapter 14

Charlotte

"Yes, Uncle, Alpha Adam showed up a few minutes after the rogue wolves did."

"That is convenient timing," her uncle responded.

"No, I don't think the two things are related." Charlotte sighed.

"I would still like to question the rogues to make sure."

Though her uncle's words were suspicious, his tone wasn't, making her wonder whether his suspicion was more a formality.

"That's why I'm calling you. To let you know two of them are currently unconscious in front of my property. I assume you want to pick them up."

"Thank you, Charlotte, I will get some pack enforcers together and we will be there in the next fifteen minutes. Are you okay to be there until then?"

She wasn't sure what her uncle was asking; whether it was being with the rogues or being alone with Adam. Rather than ask, she gave a blanket answer.

"I'll be fine, Uncle, just get here as soon as you can."

"I love you, Niece, see you in a bit."

Charlotte stepped outside about halfway through her phone call with her uncle to see Adam on his own phone call. She reminded herself that he was an alpha, which meant this sort of attack probably had to be reported. But since she was closest to her uncle's pack, though in neutral territory, she would assume it would go to them and not Adam's.

Watching him get off his own call, she prepared for that argument.

"Are you okay?" he asked her, leaning over her fence as if trying to examine her.

"I'm fine, just a couple bumps and bruises— I had worse damage last time."

When his whole body stiffened, she realized she'd said the wrong thing.

"What do you mean last time? Your uncle told me you were bothered by rogues, but he didn't say it was an all-out fight." He was gritting his teeth and there was a growl to his voice.

Wanting to tread lightly, Charlotte took a step back, even though the fence was still between them. "Rogues have been here three times. The first time, I scared them off. The second time, even blasting them didn't get them to leave. I kept attacking until they ran off."

Adam began eyeing her suspiciously. "Why didn't your magic function this time?"

Biting her lip, Charlotte debated lying. They were close enough for him to smell the lie if he had a good sense of smell. "Since gaining my wolf, my magic can sometimes be on the fritz. No one knows why, sometimes they won't work, or won't work properly. I don't accidentally shoot off magic anymore, so that's a plus."

Adam seemed more alarmed. "You're out here by yourself, with rogues running around, and your magic can sometimes be on the fritz?"

He was leaning over the fence as his temper rose, and he flinched. Charlotte looked down to see blood trailing from his left leg.

"Did one of them bite you?" she asked without thinking, interrupting his tirade.

Adam blinked a couple times as if she'd caught him off-guard. "Yes, it'll heal in a week or so." He opened his mouth to speak again.

Charlotte waved her hands back and forth. "No, no, no, you can't stand there and free-bleed. Get your butt inside the house so I can at least bandage it up." She unlocked and opened the little white front gate and motioned for him to walk in.

Letting out a growl, he walked past her, going out of his way not to brush her on his way through the gate. When she'd locked it behind him, she turned to see him holding a bouquet.

He seemed to have forgotten it, as when her attention was drawn to them, he sputtered before holding them up and handing them to her.

"I noticed how much care you put in your garden, so I brought you some flowers, along with your invitation to the ball," he muttered, clearly embarrassed.

Charlotte felt a little pang in her chest. Adam was so sweet and smelled fantastic every time she was near him.

"Thank you, they're quite pretty. I'll put them in water and then we'll bandage you up." She moved around him and up the stone path to her front door.

Adam didn't crowd her; he maintained a good two paces behind her. Meanwhile, Buster was plastered to her side.

The front door led straight into the kitchen with the living area to the left. She headed to the sink, grabbed a vase, and began filling it with water. She felt Adam standing in the doorway, scrutinizing the space. The cottage was small, but she didn't need a lot of room and Buster didn't take up much room either.

"This is quite cozy," he commented after a minute.

After placing the vase on the sill of the large window, Charlotte turned to smile at him. "Thank you, I really like it." She motioned to the small kitchen table sitting between the kitchen and living room with its two seats. "Now sit, I'm getting the first-aid kit from the bathroom."

As she moved out of the room, she swore she heard Adam chuckle. When she came back out, he was in one of the chairs, but had removed his pants. This very attractive alpha sat in her kitchen in only boxers and a T-shirt, showing off incredible runner's thighs, which Charlotte had always been partial to. She was glad his back was to her because she was sure her lusty thoughts were playing on her face before she could school it.

Once she could form a bland, reassuring smile, she came around him to plop the first-aid kit on the table. When she saw his leg, she couldn't help the intake of breath and wince. There were deep grooves from just above his knee all the way down to mid-calf.

"On second thought, I need to sit on the floor for this," Charlotte commented before moving the first-aid kit to the floor and opening it to grab the disinfecting wipes. She then sat cross-legged in front of his leg and began wiping the blood.

She heard Adam hiss but ignored it. Once she had it clean, she pulled out several large non-adhesive bandages and her medical honey. She slathered the honey on the wounds and then put each non-adhesive square up against his leg, before wrapping the medical tape around each one. She ended up using five of those pads and almost an entire spool of medical tape. But the medical honey should help to prevent infection.

"There," she said as she looked down at her handiwork. "You should be all set and able to get out of here. I wouldn't walk on it too much unless you have to. But feel free to head out, my uncle and some of his men will be here in the next ten minutes or so."

Adam crossed his arms over his chest and frowned down at her. "Don't be ridiculous, I'm not leaving you here by yourself. In fact, I don't think you should be left here by yourself even after your uncle is done."

Charlotte sputtered. "Excuse me?"

"You said yourself your magic is on the fritz, and these rogues are getting more and more bold. I don't like the idea of you being out here on your own. What would've happened if I hadn't decided to come this afternoon?" He looked down at her cocking up one eyebrow.

There was a chance she could've fought them off, but it was slim. Not that she would admit that out loud.

"They got through the wards by brute force. Now that I know they can do that, I can change the wards accordingly. I will be fine. I've been out here on my own for years."

She saw sadness in Adam's eyes at her words.

"You're staying with me. I have a large house, and I'm currently the only one in it. You and Buster will stay with me for a week or two until we figure out exactly what these rogues want. And if we don't, the Dark Falls witches will be here, and they might be able to put some more complicated wards in place." His icy, commanding tone made it clear if she continued to argue he would chuck her over his shoulder take her to his house forcefully.

Chapter 15

Charlotte

Charlotte's jaw hit the floor. They were near strangers! Sure, he was an alpha and used to protecting people, but he wasn't her alpha—it wasn't his job to protect her.

"No, thank you, if I stay with anyone, it'll be my uncle and aunt or a cousin, Not an almost complete stranger."

Anger blazed in his eyes. Charlotte had to fight the urge to back up. Every fiber of her being was sure Adam would never hurt her, though she didn't know why she had such confidence in that idea.

"You're staying with me. It will be unexpected, if they happen to know who your uncle is, because I don't know if this was a targeted attack or happened by chance. Either way, it would make more sense if you stayed with me. My house is in the middle of the pack territory, harder for them to get to. I am absolutely sure your uncle will agree with me when he gets here."

"I do believe I have a say in where I go. I do not think what I do with my life is up to various men. But thanks for the input." Anger flared through her with such force she balled her hands into fists as if to contain it.

Adam stood and finally looked away from her, sliding his pants back on, clearly putting the denim over his left leg more gingerly than his right. Once clothed again, he shoved his hands in his pockets and continued standing. He now towered over Charlotte, who still sat cross-legged on the floor.

"I realize I am not your alpha, that you don't have an alpha. But look at this logistically. They have attacked you three times; they now know how to get through your wards. If I hadn't come along, you would not have been able to defend yourself. If these wolves know you and this was a pointed attack, they know you're most likely to be with your uncle, who if memory serves, lives towards the back of the pack territory. Being that close to the border made it an easier for determined rogues to breach.

"I, on the other hand, am an alpha, have my own house, not at the edge of the territory. I am not affiliated with you or your family, which means the chances of them putting two and two together that you will be at my house are slim. And yes, I say that knowing I participated in today's fight, but that doesn't mean they recognized me or my wolf." He had his arms crossed over his chest again.

The dominating protective instincts Adam was showing made her insides flip-flop and Charlotte hated it. Trying to cover, she scrambled to her feet, closing her first-aid kit, and taking several steps back so he wouldn't be in her personal space.

"I'm not staying with a stranger. There are other people I can stay with." She mentally patted herself on the back for how calm her voice sounded. She stepped around him and headed back towards the bathroom.

As she passed, she heard Adam growling before his hand whipped out and grabbed her upper arm. "You and Buster are staying with me and that's final. Pack a bag."

Charlotte was so irritated that she wanted to slap him. Before she could think through the movement, he dropped her arm and looked away. She stormed to the bathroom and put her first-aid kit back. She stood in the bathroom staring at herself in the mirror for several seconds, trying to collect herself again.

He had a good point. She couldn't stay out here by herself anymore. She was endangering both herself and Buster. She'd just reinforced the wards a little over a week ago. They shouldn't have been able to get through. Either she hadn't enforced them as well as she thought, or they had some sort of medallion that would help them get through it. Or a witch, which seemed the least likely. Either way, she wasn't safe out here by herself; no matter the reason, they could get through. But that didn't automatically make her jump to staying with him. She was sure her uncle Ferdinand would agree with her and offer her the spare bedroom at his and her aunt's house.

While she stood in the bathroom, she heard tires rolling up around the back of the house. Relief flooded her as she exited the bathroom and headed out the back door, at the end of the hallway for the two bedrooms and one bathroom in the cottage. Adam was two steps behind her, and closing in, too close for comfort. It was as if he was afraid to be too far away from her, if the people in the vehicles turned out to be a threat.

She recognized her uncle's truck immediately and relaxed. A few seconds later, he hopped out, as did an enforcer from the passenger seat. From the van behind them, three more men Charlotte vaguely recognized exited.

"Around the front, in front of the fence," she called to the men.

Her uncle nodded and motioned for the enforcers to go around the house and check out the rogues. He went straight to the back fence and let himself in. He was greeted with her happy, waggly pup. He let out a chuckle and scratched Buster behind his ears for a second before standing and walking over to her, embracing her in a hug.

Again, she swore she heard Adam growl. She thought it was her imagination until her uncle let go, frowning at the man over her shoulder.

"Thank you for helping my niece, Alpha Adam. It's much appreciated."

"She isn't safe out here." Adam's gravelly tone was so deep the words were hard to make out.

"Yes, I agree with you, at least while these rogues are a problem." Her uncle's attention drew back to her. "I'd feel much more comfortable if you and the dog came and stayed with your aunt and me for a week or two. Maybe longer depending on this rogue problem."

"No." Adam's voice was so filled with that angry growl the word almost disappeared.

Charlotte could feel him vibrating with alpha dominance intensity behind her. It made her back itch. She took a step to the side and turned so she could see both him and her uncle.

Adam looked scary. He was seething, his wolf close to the surface. A zip of panic shot through her.

Adam must've smelled it, as his eyes shifted from her uncle to her. "I won't hurt you."

"I know that," she whispered.

He watched her another second and visibly reined himself in before turning back to her uncle Ferdinand. "She'll stay with me. If this was a targeted attack, they'll know you're her uncle and where to find her. I don't have any connection to your family. My property is better insulated than yours."

Charlotte swung her attention to her uncle, expecting him to be as outraged by the suggestion as she was. Much to her surprise, he seemed to be thinking it through.

"Uncle Ferdinand, clearly you see this for the insanity it is. There is no reason for the alpha of Valley River to be involved in this." Her voice held a twinge of panic.

Her uncle watched Adam for a beat before turning his eyes back to her, his expression softened. "Actually, he's right. They wouldn't look for you at his house. They'd look for you first at mine. Then probably Riker's. Which reminds me, I should call and give him a heads-up. He'll go ballistic about this."

Adam growled again.

"Will you stop that!" Charlotte exclaims exasperated.

The growling stopped. Adam slowly turned to her, intensity still in his gaze.

"Are you sure there's no better option, Uncle Ferdinand?" Charlotte already knew the answer, but she really hoped something else would pop up. She didn't want to stay with the strange alpha who suddenly kept growling and had brought her flowers. She didn't appreciate the territorial nature of Adam's attitude towards her. "What about Muriel?"

"I'm sorry, niece, this might be the best option. And I appreciate Alpha Adam volunteering." Her uncle sounded resigned and gave her a sad smile. "Muriel is a good fighter, but she is hot-headed and would fight before thinking the situation through."

Charlotte started to growl as she looked between the two men. Then she was momentarily distracted by the enforcers carrying the two hogtied rogue wolves around the house.

"Fine, but I'm taking my own car," Charlotte conceded before throwing up her hands and storming back into the cottage.

She was relieved when no one followed her, and she began packing two weeks' worth of stuff for both her and Buster.

When she came back out, a fourth vehicle was parked at the side of her little driveway and Charlotte wondered how close Adam had been parked that it hadn't taken him more than the time it took her to pack to get his car and come back.

When she stepped back out of the cottage, with Buster on his leash and the last of their stuff in her other hand, her uncle waved her off and hopped back into his truck. Then he and the enforcers left, leaving just her little hatchback, and Adam's SUV.

"Do you need me to take anything?" Adam asked, his tone more what she was accustomed to hearing from him.

Shaking her head, she opened the back door to let Buster jump in before putting the last of his stuff in the foot well of the back seat. "No, we're fine. I'll follow you out." She didn't even look at him as she spoke. She was so frustrated and felt so defeated about the scenario that she found herself wishing Adam hadn't shown up to the fight earlier. But as soon as that thought occurred to her, she knew it was preposterous. Who knew what would've happened if she hadn't been able to beat those three rogues by herself.

Chapter 16

One Week Later

Adam

Adam's house felt full of women. Three of Charlotte's female cousins appeared at his doorstep two hours before the ball with many bags and containers. Beyond the initial introductions, they almost bowled him over to run upstairs to the room Charlotte was staying in. It had been more than a year since there were this many people in his house.

Having her scent mingling with his this whole week had him on edge, which did not endear him to Buster. Adam and the pitbull had come to a kind of understanding over the last week. Buster stopped growling at him and in return, Adam stopped trying to bribe the dog into liking him.

Charlotte had mentioned a couple days earlier that if she was expected to go to this ball, she would need her cousin Muriel to bring the dress. Since Adam desperately wanted her to go to the ball, to have a night with her, to have her on his arm, he agreed.

Having her in his home this last week was driving him absolutely insane. Her scent was everywhere, and it was both comforting and aggravating at the same time. She should recognize his scent as her mate's scent, and they should be well on their way to strengthening a mating bond. And yet she'd all but ignored him unless she needed to speak to him until three days ago. Adam figured she was still ticked that he all but kidnapped her and her dog to his house.

He could not understand why the mating bond and the urge to make it stronger wasn't pulling at her the way it pulled at him. The more time she spent in his house, the tighter wound he became. He began snapping at people more readily than he usually did. All he wanted to do was throw Charlotte over his shoulder, take her into his bedroom, and camp out there for days. But he couldn't. For whatever reason, she wasn't acknowledging their connection and Adam didn't have it in him to force that on her. Though, he had every intention of asking Ferdinand and his wife about it at the ball tonight. He had never heard of a werewolf being able to ignore the mating bond before. And he needed more information on exactly why she was doing it and how.

Another knock at the door interrupted his thoughts, and he frowned. He could hear the women laughing upstairs as they got ready.

Hoping it wasn't a problem with the pack territory, he slowly opened the door and was surprised to see Riker standing outside.

The older man towered over him and frowned as the door opened. "Alpha Adam," he said with a clipped tone.

"Riker." He stood out of the way so Riker could enter his home.

The taller man hesitated and made a huffing noise before stepping inside and Adam closed the door behind him.

"I was originally escorting all of them. And I am not about to show up to that ball by myself. This was the best alternative." The explanation came out swift on one breath.

Honestly, Adam couldn't blame him. He'd seen the way women tended to corner Riker and he could tell the bigger man didn't like all that female attention.

"Have a seat, do you want something to drink?" Adam offered, as he waved towards the couch and stepped further into the room.

"No, thank you, I'm fine." Riker eyed Adam several moments.

Adam stared at him right back.

"You know she already has a mate, right?" This time when Riker spoke, the words were quiet.

Adam felt the growl vibrate up his throat before he could control it.

Riker watched him with interest. "So, Ferdinand's right, you are her mate. Interesting."

His tone held more curiosity than malice. That helped Adam reign control on the growl and his wolf who stalked closer to the surface of his brain.

"I don't know how she has managed to ignore this, but she is mine."

Riker slowly crossed his arms over his chest, making the arms of his suit jacket pull slightly. "Has she mentioned that you smell like home?" The words were said so carefully, as if Riker wasn't sure he wanted the answer.

This time when he growled in exasperation. "No, she seems to be ignoring it entirely."

Frowning, Riker looked at the ceiling as another round of laughter went off. "That doesn't make sense. You will be great for her."

It was a strange camaraderie Adam felt in that moment. It was as if Riker was, in his own way, accepting Adam into their little fold. Adam had always wanted a big family, ruckus people barging into his life and here he was, standing in his living room, discussing his mate with her cousin while she and other cousins got ready upstairs. It should've been a dream come true for him, and yet sorrow bloomed in his chest because for whatever reason all of this was just out of his reach.

"Maybe you need that drink," Riker commented trying to lighten the mood.

"Yeah, you might be right." Adam scoffed as he headed towards the kitchen to get himself a beer.

Chapter 17

Charlotte

The look Adam gave her as she and her cousins walked down his staircase sent her libido skyrocketing. Which was saying something, since even though she was still ticked at him for sweeping up Buster and her, being around Adam all week had stoked a fire deep in her belly, giving her some of the most erotic dreams she ever had in her life.

He appeared to be fighting the urge to pick her up and carry her back upstairs, to his own room. He recovered by the time all four of them reached the bottom, but she had seen that expression, nonetheless. He wanted her, badly, but there was a sadness underlying that want.

Charlotte recognized it because to a certain extent she felt it. As angry at him as she was for stealing her away, she really liked Adam. She felt a pull to him that made him hard to ignore. He was kind, caring, and goofy when he needed to be. His mate would be one lucky woman and part of her was angry it couldn't be her.

She thought about the idea of having a fling with Adam, but he was an alpha and she still had not decided if she would remain a recluse. A fling wouldn't last longer than staying at his house and she wasn't sure she wanted that.

Between the six of them, they piled into two vehicles. She and Adam in his SUV, along with Muriel in the back seat, the rest of her cousins in Riker's truck.

The drive to the pack house was full of Muriel making inappropriate jokes and Charlotte absolutely loved it. She found herself cackling along with her cousin and she even heard Adam chuckle a couple times.

By the time they got to the pack house, the parking lot was half full. As they stepped out, Muriel made a joke about hoping there were more single, attractive werewolves this year than there had been last. Adam snorted and said something under his breath neither of them heard, which was probably for the best.

Riker pulled in next to them. As a group, they started walking towards the front door ... until hearing the shrill ring that meant Riker had gotten a text. Then another came from her other side where she assumed Adam's phone sat in his pocket. They all exchanged glances as both men took their phones out.

"Did you get a text from your alpha asking to meet in the parking lot really quick before the blessing ceremony?" Adam asked Riker, looking up from his phone.

Her cousin frowned and nodded. "Yeah, he said to meet in the corner where there aren't any cars so we can't be overheard."

The two of them exchanged wary glances before Adam tapped something out on his phone and looked at Charlotte and her female cousins.

"Why don't you ladies go inside? We'll meet you as soon as this whole thing is done," Adam suggested, gesturing towards the pack house.

"Absolutely not," Muriel chimed in. "I put money on this being about those rogues and that affects Charlotte a lot more than it affects the rest of us. She deserves to hear what's going on. Even if she must be a couple steps off so you can have your alpha meeting." She waved her arms back and forth as she said the last part. "She can at least hear what happened immediately after and plan accordingly. I'll even stand with her so she's not by herself."

This was why Charlotte loved Muriel. She was never afraid to state her opinion.

Both Riker and Adam frowned at that proposal.

"Look, boys, frown if you want, but we're going to follow you out, so this is a waste of time." Muriel motioned towards the back part of the lot where they were supposed to meet Alpha Alexander.

Adam growled loudly in protest.

Muriel smirked at him. "Look, I'm just telling the truth. We can walk in there with our cousins, but we'll be walking back out two seconds later. We might as well be honest about the whole scenario."

"Don't argue with them. It's better not to argue with them when there's several of them on the same side." Riker sighed before pivoting in the gravel lot and heading in the direction they were supposed to meet.

Adam let out something between a growl and yell before turning and following Riker.

"He's spicy. I like that," Muriel cooed when Adam was out of hearing distance.

A spike of possessive jealousy shot through Charlotte, even though she had absolutely no claim to him.

"Oh, that was an interesting reaction, Charlotte," her cousin cooed at her as they began walking.

"Oh, shut up, Muriel." Charlotte sighed.

Muriel chuckled but didn't respond.

As they walked across the lot, Adam and Riker were soon joined by Ferdinand and his alpha, Carson. When they weaved between the cars to come stand beside the other men, Muriel and Charlotte exchanged glances. Nothing good could come from this particular group meeting right before one of the biggest festivities of the year.

As the group reached the corner of the parking lot and stopped, Muriel and Charlotte several yards from the main group, Muriel scented the surrounding air.

"Char, do you smell that?" she whispered so the dominant wolves wouldn't hear her.

Charlotte was shaking her head before the answer left her lips. "No, you know I don't have as good of a sense of smell as most werewolves. Something to do with the witch genetics. I only scent slightly better than humans do. What smell?"

Charlotte watched the group warily as it looked like Riker and Ferdinand were scenting the air as well, probably smelling whatever Muriel was talking about.

"It smells like there are more wolves here. As if there were a group of wolves, or a group of wolves just left. I don't recognize them all."

Paranoia started to crawl up from Charlotte stomach. But before she could recommend they leave, there was rustling from the trees beside the lot to the left and all of them turned to see Alpha Alexander exiting the tree line, along with a group of seven other wolves, one of which, she was surprised to see was Brian.

"What the hell is this?" Muriel gasped as she grabbed Charlotte's arm and started backing them farther away from the wooded area.

The two women were lucky, as they were much farther from the approaching group than the men were.

"Oh no, I'm willing to bet this is Brian's reaction to finding out Riker replaced him as the next alpha of the pack."

Charlotte fought the instinct to move forward and help fight. She wasn't a strong fighter, and she needed to remember that.

Alpha Alexander looked worse for wear, as if he had been ambushed before the others got there. Which would make sense considering the texts supposedly came from his phone.

"Thank you for making this all so easy for us," Brian's voice slithered with smugness.

"Son, what exactly are you doing?" growled Carson in response.

Brian snapped at the older alpha. "I'm not your son, old man, and only this one's son because of genetics." As he pointed to his father, he snapped and the two men holding him tossed him towards the group.

Charlotte winced as Alpha Alexander skidded across the gravel lot, clearly unable to control his own fall. She itched to step forward and help get him out of the fray, but she was not about to stand between the two groups.

"All the big alphas in this section of the world, all in one place. You're making our job easy, aren't they, boys?" He snapped again as he finished, and four more snarling hulking werewolves stepped out of the tree line.

There was now eleven of them, probably the rogue faction they had been dealing with, and only five standing opposite them. Seven, counting herself and Muriel. Muriel was a decent fighter, but both were in dresses which weren't exactly easy to fight in, unless they shifted.

The odds were not good. Adrenaline shot through her and she could feel magic sparking down her arms to her fingertips. If she tapped her fingers together sparks would start flying. Ever since the change, her magic had been tied more to her emotions. For once, it might work to Charlotte's advantage.

She watched as Brian and his lackeys stalked toward the group of alphas and betas. She would only have the element of surprise once, so she needed to use it wisely, it would blow her secret, not just for her but everyone who helped her keep it, putting all of them at the alphas' mercy. But she couldn't stand idly by while Riker and Adam got hurt. She would never forgive herself if she put her secret over their safety. She began pushing her power towards her hands, letting it build and build like static electricity.

"Muriel, step away from me," she whispered loud enough for only Muriel to hear.

Brian was still talking, and so far, ignoring the two females.

Muriel looked wide-eyed down at Charlotte's hands before taking two enormous steps back towards the building.

That seemed to get Brian's attention for the first time, as well as some of his lackeys. He cocked his head toward Charlotte and Muriel.

"Well, if it isn't the thorn in my side," he snarled as his eyes bore into Charlotte.

"Don't talk to her!" Adam snarled.

"You have some nerve." Ferdinand snapped at the same time.

Brian ignored them and continued to stare at Charlotte. "Why is it you're always around to make things more difficult?"

Truly perplexed by Brian's statement, Charlotte opened her mouth, closed it again, then repeated that twice before finally stringing some words together.

"I think out of the two of us, you made my life much more difficult than I've made yours." It wasn't a smart thing to say, but it was true.

He sneered at her and took a step in her direction. She saw Adam tense.

"Once I take care of these pathetic would-be alphas and take over their packs for myself, you won't be a problem for me anymore." His smile was predatory.

Anger started twining through her like a vine, taking over, enhancing the magic and dousing the fear. "That's your big problem, Brian, you have a lot of confidence and that makes you underestimate those around you. If you had actually gotten to know me, you would realize you didn't have the upper hand you thought you had."

As Brian blinked at her, perplexed, she screamed.

It was raw magic, powerful, and didn't have the best aim. But she couldn't remember an exact spell for the type of magic she needed. She threw up her hands palms out and aimed them at the rogue wolves. A blast of pure force hit all of them, hard, knocking four of them headfirst into thick tree trunks, effectively knocking them out.

The remaining seven were dazed. Brian and the biggest of his goons started getting up first.

"Now!" Ferdinand yelled. Taking advantage of their opponents' stunned states, the five men jumped into the fray.

Knowing she wouldn't be able to get a blast like that off again, with how erratic her power was, Charlotte started moving closer. She could hear Muriel's protests, but her ears were fuzzy from her scream, so she ignored it. Stepping to the edge of the parking lot, Charlotte shook her hands to amass as much power in them as she could manage, scanning the scene in front of her to figure out which target would best suit their side.

"No," she called, as one of the stunned goons launched himself at Alpha Carson's back.

The blast hit him in the side of the chest sending him tumbling over, clipping Carson in the shoulder, but rolling the man on top of Carson's opponent.

"Appreciate it," Carson called over his shoulder without looking away from his two opponents. He then grabbed the bigger goon by the neck and begin throttling, using that werewolf strength, until it was clear the other man was knocked out.

"I got a hold of Ivan, he's grabbing some wolves and heading here now," Muriel yelled in order to be heard over the growling and snarling.

Ivan was Crescent Falls's beta. A tough man in his early forties who was deadly in every fight he'd ever been in.

Seeming to sense he'd quickly be outnumbered, Brian took several steps back from the fight as if to flee, leaving his men behind.

"Oh, no you don't," Charlotte called and threw out her hands at him.

This time though, her power fizzled, and she felt the energy leave her hands in a puff of smoke.

"Dammit," she murmured and tried again.

Brian grinned maniacally. He then took another few steps before launching himself in the air and landing right beside her. She had gotten even closer to the fight without meaning to. Before she could fully process how close he was, he had her head-locked, knife against her throat.

Chapter 18

Charlotte

"You leave my men and me alone or I'm slicing the hybrid's pretty little throat since she seems to matter to several of you more than her worth."

The fighting stopped, though there were only four enemy combatants still conscious, not including Brian.

She heard Ferdinand growling, and saw Adam fighting down his wolf, his breathing ragged, his growl was deeper, more menacing than her uncle's.

"I will murder you in your sleep if I have to," Adam snarled as he took two large steps towards them.

She felt the knife prick her neck and her eyes went glassy with unshed tears.

"Ah, ah, ah, no moving any closer. I want all of you to stand behind dear Muriel there and let us leave in peace."

"How can you do this; you're supposed to be that girl's alpha some day?" Her uncle snarled, as he began following Brian's instructions.

There was a snort and a cackle from behind her and unshed tears fell, it didn't matter how much she tried to fight them.

"Who gave you that idea? Alexander? The old man is gullible and stupid."

The alpha in question was sitting up now, though clearly still dazed. He looked at his son, utterly bewildered.

Her eyes found Muriel's and her cousin shifted her eyes over Brian's shoulder. Charlotte remembered Ivan was getting back up. If she could distract Brian long enough, maybe someone would come up behind them. She just needed to throw him off. The problem would be his cronies, who would see anyone coming.

"You kept being where my meetings were years ago. I started this rogue group, now three dozen strong, and we had to meet in secret, at odd places and times. You always seemed to show up there. In the end, it made you a good alibi. And a good distraction. Until my father took it too seriously."

Bewilderment flooded her. Brian used his father's misunderstanding as cover, a decoy so he could have his coup. It was why he had not outright denied it when his father asked all those years ago.

The growl started deep in her throat and before Brian could do more than register it, she sent up her leg, fast and hard, right into his crotch. She twisted her arm under his to push the knife away from her neck.

Once again, he'd underestimated her, seeing her as no threat despite her proving otherwise. Brian dropped the knife and his arm as she pushed him; the shot to the crotch also helped. As he started to back up, she pivoted and punched him as hard as she could in the face. Blood rocketed from his nose as he bent over.

Regretting wearing heels, Charlotte kneed him in the head.

Before she could get another blow in, strong male arms wrapped around her waist, lifting her off the ground as two others came around to snatch up Brian. She could make out that one of them was Ivan, who was barking orders for them to get the rest of the rogues in line for the small crowd of werewolves behind him.

"Shhh, Shhh, it's okay now, I've got you," Adam whispered in her ear.

She realized she was still growling and snarling and forced herself to take a large shaky breath.

"There you go, remind me never to get on your bad side," he teased.

She could feel his breath fluttering across her skin, and her body converted the anger to more positive and steamy use.

Adam took a deep breath and let out a growl against her neck, only making matters worse.

He moved away from her and set her down. But he didn't move more than half a step away. Instead, he came around her front, holding her shoulders, his eyes boring into hers.

"I'm going to kiss you, now is the time to tell me not to if you're against it."

Charlotte let out a shaky breath. "Definitely not against it."

Then came that sexy growl again, and he yanked her to him, smashing his mouth to hers. Fireworks exploded behind her closed lids and cascaded through her brain. She gasped, and he used the opportunity to dip his tongue inside, kissing her more passionately and more skillfully than Charlotte had ever been kissed.

It was a mate's first kiss. The fireworks were the telltale sign, the confirmation one really found their mate.

When he finally pushed back, clearly dragging himself away, his hands dropped to caress her arms instead of holding onto her.

"You do not know how long I've been waiting for that."

"How did you—? Why? You knew?" So many thoughts were floating around her head, Charlotte couldn't keep them straight.

"Of course, I knew, from the first time I scented you, I knew you were home for me. I kept waiting for you to notice the same thing. But you never acknowledged it."

Shaking her head, she laughed. "I don't have a werewolf sense of smell. It's one of those things about having witch blood too. I can't do all witchy things and I can't do all werewolf things. Don't get me wrong—you smell absolutely fantastic. But there's no click in the brain like you seem to have."

Adam dropped one of his hands and ran it through his tussled hair. "Of course, you can't, and if I had brought it up, this probably could've been cleared up a week ago."

Charlotte was pretty sure that statement was more aimed towards him than her, so she stayed quiet.

"Carson, if you're okay taking charge of the scene, I'll take my mate to meet the witches and see if there's something they can do about helping her harness her magic better. We can have a meeting next week about mopping up what is left of these rogues."

His hand made a lazy journey down her arm until they clasped hands.

Charlotte turned to look toward the green area to see Carson standing, grinning like an idiot at both of them. "Of course, if you wouldn't mind sending your beta out here so we can put them in your jail cells, given those are closest, that would be most helpful. I'm certainly not opposed to you playing hooky to help the woman that saved me from getting ambushed." He gave Charlotte a kind smile and inclined his head.

She blushed.

"His second's already here, Ivan grabbed him," from the far end of the group, a man with a dark ponytail said. He checked the pulse of one of the wolves she initially knocked out. He turned to Adam, smiling lopsidedly. "I'll take care of it, boss. But uh, you and I will have a conversation about this later." He motioned between Adam and Charlotte.

She turned back to see Adam grunt and roll his eyes before tugging her hand so she would follow him.

"Oh, there's no way I'm missing this," Muriel quipped as they passed her, and she fell in step aside Charlotte.

Charlotte laughed and leaned in close to Adam, taking in his scent, letting it overwhelm her senses. "And to think, I was so jealous of your future mate."

A devilish grin curled his lips as he turned and looked at her. "Were you now? Well Luna, I suppose we can go into greater detail about that, and all the reasons you might've been jealous, when we get home tonight."

When he said the word 'home', pleasant little tingles shot through her.

"Maybe I'll keep those to myself. Wouldn't want you to get a big head this early on."

Adam chuckled. "You're lucky your cousin is here; it prohibits the number of innuendos I'm willing to make."

"Oh, don't stop on my account, alpha boy. I'll be making them right along with you," Muriel responded with a smile.

Adam let out a mock groan and pretended to wince. "What have I gotten myself into?"

"Probably more love, fun, and good-natured animosity than you've ever had in your life." Charlotte giggled.

This time his affection for her filled his eyes and took her breath away. "And I absolutely cannot wait." He squeezed her hand as they headed to the ball, full of wolves unaware of the goings-on out in the parking lot.

About the Author

Gretchen spawned in the Puget Sound region. After some wandering she returned there and now lives with her husband and the daintiest Rottweiler on the planet. When not drowning herself in coffee, as is custom in the Greater Seattle Area, Gretchen can be found at her day job or sitting at her desk in the home office, flailing her arms as she dictates to her computer.

If you enjoyed this book, please feel free to leave a review on the site of a retailer of your choice. Reviews are always appreciated.

You can find Gretchen at:

Gretchens.b.author@gmail.com
Gretchensb.com
Facebook.com/authorGretchenSB
Tiktok.com/@gretchensb

Turn the page to find out more about Gretchen's other series.

Scent of Home Series

A werewolf knows their mate when they smell them. The smell is said to be like coming home. And though that means something different to everyone it's always unmistakable. While finding one's mate might be easy keeping them is another story.

Each book has different main characters, though the members of the community keep popping up in other books. The heat level is low, with usually just kissing, with more happening off-page.

Alpha's Magical Mate

Night World Series

These paranormal romances take place in a world with warriors, werecreatures, immortals, and magical practitioners. A rebellious plot may be coming to North America but that isn't stopping fate from putting the Night World inhabitants in the paths of their mates.

Each book has different main characters, though the members of the community keep popping up in other books.

Trigger Warnings: Some light fight scenes, kidnapping, consensual adult scenes.

Lady of the Dead
Viking Sensitivity
A Wolf in Cop's Clothing
Hidden Shifter
Visions Across the Veil

Berman's Wolves Trilogy

While in college an experiment goes horribly wrong and hundreds of students are turned into werewolves. Now years later these werewolves struggle to survive on their own as strange scientists try to take them for experimentation one by one. The more they dig into those scientists, the bigger their problems seem to be. Even their own are keeping secrets and could change everything.

Trigger Warnings: Some mild fight scene.

Berman's Wolves
Berman's Chosen
Berman's Secret
Berman's Origin *(A companion Novella)*

Anthony Hollownton Series

Anthony Hollownton is a workaholic homicide detective. When a case has him stumbling into the supernatural world, he finds it hard to believe. Even when he finds familiar faces. He wants no part of it and they don't want him there either. Yet case after case he's pulled back in.

Trigger Warnings: Some light fight scenes, graphic crime scenes.

Hollownton Homicide
Hollownton Outsiders
Hollownton Legacy
Hollownton Case File *(A companion Novella)*

Jas Bond Series

Jas owns a supernatural antique store he inherited from his mother. Though as a magicless son of the witch he doesn't always have a lot in common with his customers. All Jas wants is to live a quiet life with Bailey his goofy Rottweiler and run the store. But the characters who come into his shop keep yanking him back into trouble.

Trigger Warnings: Some light fight scenes.

Green Goo Goblin
Spectacle Stealing Supernatural
Book Burgling Blood Magic
Antique Absconding Arsonist
Property Pilfering Pariah

Lantern Lake Series

The holiday season is a big one for lantern Lake. Though the lake is surrounded by three small towns their holiday festival is something people come to see from all over the state. Not only does winter bring that holiday festival but it usually brings love along with it.

Each book has different main characters, though the members of the community keep popping up in other books. The heat level is low, with usually just kissing.

Pizza Pockets and Puppy Love
A flurry of Feelings
Teacher's Crush
Pugs and Peppermint Sticks
Moving Home for the Holidays
Mayor May Not
Building a Holiday Miracle

Forest's Edge Series

Forest's Edge doesn't exactly have much opportunity for a shifter to meet their mate, but sometimes their mates are where they least expect them.

Each book has different main characters, though the members of the community keep popping up in other books. The heat level is low, there is some on the page foreplay.

Grizzly Secret
Grizzly Plot
Grizzly Festivities
Grizzly Theft
Grizzly Kiss

Kenny's Diner Series

The pay at Kenny's Diner was too good to be true. The night shift seems to bring out everything a little strange. Kathy's pretty sure all the customers are supernatural creatures. But some are a little too hard to explain. It's a good thing this gig pays so well.

Kenny's diner is an episodic series following Kathy, a human server, working at a 24-hour diner that's a hub of supernatural activity.

Don't trust a wolf in a leather vest
Don't get between a dog and his cheese
It May Be Tasty, But it's Still a Bad Idea
You can't see the food through the trees
Have no debt remain outstanding
Not all grandmas are trustworthy
Ignore the rainbow
Let's not make a deal
It's all fun and games until someone loses a pie
Sports are the leading cause of death

Made in the USA
Columbia, SC
22 November 2024